PERIL IN PENSACOLA

ACCIDENTALLY UNDERCOVER MYSTERIES - BOOK 1

LUCY QUINN

CONTENTS

Cover by Lewellen Designs

Editing by Angie Ramey

ABOUT THIS BOOK

Peril in Pensacola
Accidentally Undercover Mysteries - Book 1

Dora Winslow is having a hard day. Not only does she stumble upon a money laundering scheme, but the next thing she knows her boss is dead. As the prime suspect for his murder, she goes to Brian, a police officer she trusts. She soon learns things aren't adding up because Brian's got a mysterious scheme of his own.

With her best friend, Evie by her side, Dora is on the run. But before they can leave town to secure the evidence that could clear her name, she has to bring Brian down. With help from a hot chef, a friendly mailman, and a little white dog, Dora and Evie must balance the scales to save their bottom line.

1

Dora Winslow crunched on a raw broccoli floret as she frowned at the spreadsheet before her. Landing a job as an accountant for Two to Mango, a popular Florida restaurant chain, was like a dream come true, especially when she discovered her office would be located on the top floor of the Asian fusion restaurant on the main strip of Pensacola Beach.

But the icing on the cake was that when she opened her window, the cool ocean breeze often wafted in, followed by the sound of the crashing waves on the powdery white sand of the beach. Although at the moment it was too hot for that, and she was enjoying the chill of the air-conditioning instead. What she hadn't planned on was what having delicious food just two flights below her office would do to her waistline.

A carrot gave an unsatisfying snap as she bit it, and she wished she was eating the crisp, lightly-fried calamari with mango dipping sauce the restaurant was famous for. Her frown became a full-fledged scowl as she puzzled over why the Pensacola location's marketing budget was more than ten times higher than the other restaurants in the chain.

The chain was owned by Steve Franklin, and his son Marco was the manager of the Pensacola location. Dora was used to Marco having more perks than the other managers. He was the kind of guy who led a flashy lifestyle and who didn't like to take no for an answer. Fortunately for Dora, her hair was too brown and her figure too average to capture his attention, but it explained why his expense account was more lenient than his counterparts.

Even so, the nepotism didn't explain Marco's unusually large marketing budget, and Dora's thoughts headed into criminal territory when she recalled an accounting conference session on how to spot money laundering in the service industry. It was what prompted her to want to dig further.

She considered sharing with her boss the troubling news about his son. Steve was a man whose ambition Dora respected. His success was an inspiring American-dream story of a boy who went from washing dishes to help his family get by to becoming a restaurant mogul in the state of Florida. But Steve also had a temper, and imagining how he would react to finding out his son was involved in something like a money laundering scheme broke her heart, and Dora wanted to be absolutely sure she had her facts straight before she did anything.

Her veggie plate scraped across her desk as she pushed it aside. What she needed was more information, and she knew how to get it. Marco's office was two doors down, giving her easy access to his computer. Dora could smell the odor of onions cooking just like every late afternoon before Two to Mango opened for dinner, and she knew Marco would be down on the dining room floor for the next few hours, leaving her plenty of time to do some investigating.

Her practical ballet flats padded softly over the hallway carpeting as Dora made her way to Marco's office and let herself in. The scent of his overbearing cologne lingered in the air, making her crinkle her nose as she seated herself in his chair and opened his laptop. The moment the screen lit up she sighed. His computer was password protected, but Dora was not one to give up easily. She tried a few combinations that came to her, like his birthday, his mother's maiden name, and even his vanity license plate which read *HOTSTUF*. She was drawing a blank, but she knew someone who could probably spout off ideas until she lost her voice.

Dora grabbed her phone to call Evie, her polar opposite in so many ways, but also her lifelong best friend. Evie didn't answer with hello, instead saying, "Calling me during office hours? Tell me you're sampling drinks for the new menu, and I'll be right there."

Dora smiled at her friend's eternal happiness. She was definitely Dora's sun on the dark days, and she was thankful to have such a friend. "I wish, Evie." She picked up a pen from Marco's desk and rolled it between her fingers. "I need some help. Hypothetically, of course."

"Of course."

"Say someone wanted to figure out a password for a certain restaurant manager who drives a black BMW convertible."

"You mean Marco?" Evie asked.

"Yes. A guy like him."

"Start with boobs."

"Boobs?" Dora asked skeptically, but her fingers were already moving on the keyboard.

"Trust me. It's the only thing he sees," Evie said, and Dora chuckled because her friend was right. Whenever Marco saw Evie, he'd home in on her sizeable breasts. Evie made a *hmm* sound, indicating she was thinking. "Try boobs, one. Or boobs one, two or—wait. How about boobs to mango? Boobs to touch?"

"My god, who are you, Evie?" Dora asked, amazed at her

friend's imagination. The keys were clicking with the flurry of Dora's fast fingers as Evie continued to spit out password options. But nothing was working until Evie said, "Boobs for me using the number four."

"Boobs4me," Dora repeated as she typed. The password box disappeared. "I'm in!"

"Hypothetically," Evie reminded her.

"Right," Dora said as she brought up the list of Marco's folders.

"I'm a hypothetical genius. You should probably bring me an order of crab cakes when you get out of work. I'm feeling the need for margarita Tuesday."

Dora was only half listening as she noticed a series of files that began with the words *Washing Machine*. She corrected her friend, who didn't always have a handle on life's little details. "Evie, it's Thursday."

"Goodie! Only two days until my birthday. This is perfect. You can get snookered with me tonight to celebrate and tomorrow give casual Friday new meaning."

Dora ignored her friend's suggestion of showing up to work hungover the next day. Even if it was Evie's milestone thirtieth birthday. She knew whatever they did for Evie would set the precedent for her thirtieth that would follow two months later. "Holy ..." Dora's jaw dropped when she clicked on the file named *Washing Machine1* and discovered a ledger for a sleazy adult book store in town. One that showed a whole lot of cash coming in. Unless dildos had become as expensive as designer handbags and shoes, there was no way the business could be having the kind of volume she was seeing. "Evie, I've got to go."

"Don't forget my crab cakes!"

Dora didn't bother to reply before she hung up. They both knew that not only would she show up for margarita Tuesday on a Thursday, she'd bring Evie her crab cakes too. She moved on to the next *Washing Machine* folder, not the least bit amused by Marco's attempt at humor, to find he was also cooking the books at a strip club, an hourly rate motel, an alligator park, and a dive bar.

Her stomach rolled with her recently consumed crudité, and she pulled open a desk drawer in search of one of the flash drives bearing the restaurant logo that someone had ordered in bulk as swag a few years ago. Clicking the orange device into the laptop, she proceeded to download the *Washing Machine* folders onto it.

As she waited, she wondered how best to inform Steve of his son's crimes. Family could be tricky, and she knew that Steve didn't see Marco the way others did. He was proud of his son, and she'd need to be careful how she approached the sticky situation.

When the files finished downloading, Dora closed Marco's laptop and left to go back to her office. She'd only taken a few steps before she heard the thudding steps of someone coming down the hallway behind her. She closed her fist tight around the thumb drive as her heart began to beat faster. There were three options as to who was behind her: Lindy, the older woman who was the executive assistant; Marco, who was busy in the restaurant; or Steve.

Dora scurried into her office and quickly sat at her desk just before Steve came in. She glanced up at him and tried her best to give him a casual, "Hey," as if she'd been sitting there the whole time.

Not only did Steve not buy her attempt at appearing unfazed by his presence, but his eyes were narrowed as if he was more than concerned. "Were you just in Marco's office?" he asked.

Dora felt her cheeks begin to heat with the shame of being chided. It wasn't an emotion she'd ever felt with Steve, although she'd certainly seen his wrath demonstrated to careless restaurant staff or to Lindy when she'd made a mistake.

But Dora didn't make mistakes. In fact, she'd been Steve's darling since the first week she'd started work and waltzed into his office to present the man with significant new tax deductions she'd found.

Dora wasn't sure why he would be annoyed with her for being in Marco's office, but seeing his anger directed toward her for the first time shook Dora's belief that she was invincible. He definitely wasn't going to take it well when she told him about Marco's schemes, and suddenly she was certain she needed hide what she'd done. She grabbed the open padded envelope sitting on her desk that she'd been preparing to send to Evie. Her friend loved getting packages, so Dora made it a point to send her one on her birthday every year to help make the day special. She slipped her hand into the bubble mailer, pretending to smooth out the tissue paper-wrapped scarf, and deposited the thumb drive as she mustered the calmest voice she could manage. "I was in Marco's office," she admitted to Steve.

"What for?"

Dora's hands shook a little as she peeled the tape off the sticky section of the envelope and sealed it, but not because she was afraid. She was upset that he'd assumed she was up to no good. She looked right into Steve's eyes to challenge him back. Even though she hated to be wrong or make someone unhappy with her, she hated criminal behavior more. And she realized she was going to have to tell the man the truth no matter what his reaction might be.

Dora stood up and placed her palms on her desk. "I was looking for his marketing budget. My records show that it's ten times that of the other restaurants, and I wanted to see his version to make sure I had my numbers right."

A soft knock on her open door made both of them turn their

attention to Lindy. "I'm leaving for the day. Did you want me to mail Evie's present for you?"

Lindy drove by the post office to get home each day, and she often took mail with her when she left work. Dora gave her a bigger smile than usual and grabbed the package to hand it to the older woman. "Thank you, Lindy. I appreciate it."

"No problem. See you both tomorrow," she said in a cheerful voice.

The woman's quick retreat told Dora she also knew Steve wasn't happy. When she saw a muscle twitch along her boss's jaw, the confidence Dora had felt about correcting a wrong slipped away, and the icy fingers of fear tripped down her spine.

"You think my son is stealing?"

"I didn't say that. I'm sure there's an explanation."

Steve raised his eyebrows at her in a way that made Dora think he didn't believe a word she'd said. It occurred to her that he was acting a lot like someone who had something to hide and that he had no intention of letting Dora find it. She had a feeling her weekend was about to start early.

E vie Grant hummed to herself as she flipped through an *In Style* magazine. Her latest job at Price Dry Cleaners was perfect for catching up on the latest trends. Perched on the counter while waiting for a customer, she bounced her foot to the beat of the song playing on the sound system. She paused for a moment to admire her shoes. She'd bought them with her last paycheck, leaving very little to pay her bills, but she knew she'd eventually catch up.

Evie twisted her foot back and forth to inspect the bright-yellow leather lace-up with a chunky heel and a white wing-tip design similar to the classic men's shoe style. Paired with her daisy print sundress that had a flouncy skirt, she was a modern version of a nineteen-fifties pin-up girl. Although, instead of the hair sprayed version of an updo, she had a pile of messy blond curls on her head with a few strands refusing to behave.

The bell on the door made Evie hop off the counter to assist the young woman who had come in. Evie let out a small noise of disapproval at the girl's outfit. While the customer was young enough to pull off the short dress that clung to every dip and valley of her body, she had a winter-palette skin tone and was wearing an autumn color.

"Honey," Evie said as she shook her head. She waved her hand as if she was scanning the woman's body with it. "Great dress, but a true red would be a much better color for you than salmon orange."

"What?" The girl glanced down at her body. "But it's my favorite color."

"And a great one to love," Evie said. "But it does nothing for your complexion." She did understand how hard it was to give up on a favorite thing, so Evie smiled and added, "Save it for your accessories. Imagine a tangerine clutch and shoes with navy blue. Divine!" she exclaimed, quite pleased with her sudden burst of brilliance. "But trust me on this; no more orange near your face, got it?"

The girl smiled. "Okay." Then she frowned. "But what should I do with this dress?"

Evie smiled back. "Size four?"

"Uh-huh."

"It'd fit me." Evie held up her palm. "Or you could give it to Goodwill. Either one works." She then tilted her head as she got to business. "Name for the pickup?"

"Danvers," the girl said, and items clattered on the counter as she emptied her purse searching for something.

Evie clicked the conveyor button on, and the machine hummed as she rotated the Ds forward. She riffled through the bags until she found an order for Danvers. "Carrie?" she asked reading off the name on the ticket. She noticed the girl was checking herself out in a compact mirror.

"Yes," said the girl.

The hangers clacked on a metal hang bar by the register when Evie hung the girl's clothing, and she entered the amount due into the register. "Cash or charge? Cash gets you a discount," she said as she'd been trained to do with every customer who didn't look like they were a lawyer or the police. Apparently, that statement raised red flags for an audit according to her boss, Fred.

After Carrie paid, she tore the plastic wrap off her order and tugged a green dress off a hanger. She held the garment up to her chest and asked, "What about this one?"

"Fabulous. You're a winter, so true jewel tones are totally you."

Carrie grinned. "Can I use your bathroom?"

"Sure, it's right over here," Evie said as she let her behind the counter. "You're going to love how that color combined with your dark hair is really going to make your skin glow."

Less than a minute later, Carrie emerged from the restroom and handed Evie the orange dress. "You were right. I look so much better in this color."

"You really do."

Carrie impulsively stepped forward and hugged Evie. "Thank you."

"Happy to help." Evie chuckled as the girl released her, and satisfaction filled her with a warm glow when Carrie left looking better than she had when she'd come into the cleaners.

"I love this job," Evie said as she held out her new acquisition to inspect it. And she discovered not only had she scored a new dress, but it was an Alexander McQueen, which cost a small fortune and was more than her credit card could hope to handle. She let out a squeal. Evie knew just what she was wearing to margarita Tuesday on this Thursday night.

"Evie!" called out Fred Price, a short, stout man who happened to own the place. "Please tell me you didn't just con another customer out of her clothing."

"I didn't! She gave it to me and even thanked me for taking it." Evie squinted her eyes at Fred. He had a surveillance camera set up to monitor the reception area. Supposedly for safety reasons, but Evie wasn't so sure that was why. "Don't you have anything better to do than spy on me from your office?" she asked as the bell rang to announce another customer's arrival.

Fred let out a low growl of frustration as Evie quickly greeted the new customer. Evie pasted on a show-stopping smile and said, "Hello. Welcome to Price Cleaners! How can I help you?"

It was a woman with a small boy, and Evie knew just how to make the child's day. When the woman said she was there to pick up the Parker order, Evie looked at the little boy. "I'm Evie. What's your name?"

"Spencer."

"Spencer, I'm going to need your help to get your Mom's clothes. Do you think you can help me?"

Spencer nodded.

"Great. So, see this big conveyor belt? It can only be turned on with"—Evie darted her eyes to the left and right as if she was afraid to reveal a secret and lowered her voice—"magic." Spencer's eyes widened. "And you're the one who has it."

He shook his head. "No, I don't."

"I think you do." Evie moved over to the conveyor and placed herself next to it so that the boy couldn't see the switch. "I want you to hold out both your hands and stare really hard at the machine. Using your mind, tell it to start."

Spencer looked up at his mother, who was smiling. She said, "Go ahead, honey."

The boy scrunched up his face and held out his hands. "Move, machine!" he called out.

Evie hit the On button with her shoulder, and the conveyor whirled to life. "You did it!" She gave Spencer a look of exaggerated shock. "I knew you were magic." She turned to Fred, who had been watching the whole thing. "Did you see that?"

Fred rolled his eyes at Evie before saying to Spencer, "That was amazing. I could use a man like you. When you're old enough for a job, come see me." He muttered under his breath to Evie. "Because I'm about to have an opening."

But Evie knew her performance meant he wasn't going to fire her. She was good with people, and he knew it. Once Spencer and his mother left, Fred said, "You're lucky you're so good with kids. You can keep your job one more day."

Evie really did have a gift for dealing with people, and she knew just what Fred needed to feel good about his decision. She grabbed his hands and gushed, "Thank you, Fred. You won't regret it."

"Humph," he grumbled as he pulled away from her. "And no more magazines. Make a dent in the phone calls to overdue orders instead."

"Will do!" Evie said with a salute.

Fred returned to his office, and she reached under the counter to grab the stack of tickets for orders that had been waiting for more than a month. It was her job to call and remind customers to pick up their garments. She only made it through four reminders when an older woman in her late sixties walked in clutching her handbag as if someone had just tried to rip it form her grip.

"Miss Nancy, how nice to see you again today. Did you forget something?" Evie asked, smiling at the woman. Miss Nancy was a regular who was in every week without fail and almost never brought in the same thing twice.

"No. I didn't forget anything." Miss Nancy thrust a bright blue Post It note at Evie, her hand shaking slightly. Her lips were pursed, causing her bright red lipstick to crack. "Did you leave this in my pocket?"

Evie glanced down at her own handwriting and nodded. "I know it's hard to keep up with fashion trends, so I figured I'd give you a heads-up before you wore that sequin blazer again. It's cute in an unexpected way, but the cut isn't quite right for your body type and the fur on the cuffs and collar... Well, I think we can all agree that mink isn't exactly socially acceptable anymore."

"This note says my jacket makes me look like a disco ball that needs a haircut!"

Evie glanced down at the blue piece of paper and bit down on her bottom lip. She'd been in a bad mood when she'd left the unsolicited advice, and it was glaringly obvious she'd gone too far because Miss Nancy was craning her neck, peeking into the back area, no doubt looking for Fred. "Uh, it was just a little humor. Of course, you would never look like a disco ball. With that tiny waist, I'm sure you're the envy of the bridge club."

"I don't play bridge," Miss Nancy snapped. "What, do you think I'm eighty?"

"Of course not," Evie said quickly, trying to recover. "You couldn't possibly be a day over forty-five."

Miss Nancy snorted. "Nice try, little lady. But it's too late to clean up this mess. I checked the pockets of my other garments and found a ton of unsolicited notes on everything from hemlines to unflattering colors." The woman raised her voice as she added, "Do you have any idea who I am?"

Evie shook her head. She just knew the woman as an eccentric lady who always showed up with interesting clothes that never quite hit the mark for Evie. "I was just trying to be helpful," Evie said nervously. Maybe she had gone too far. But when Miss Nancy hadn't commented on the notes before, Evie thought maybe she liked the advice. "Fashion is sort of my passion and—"

"*Your* passion?" Miss Nancy let out a huff of laughter and swept her gaze over Evie. "That dress is a bad knockoff from the Donna Karan line six or seven years ago. And the pants you had on last week? They had so many wrinkles they looked like you'd fished them out of a Cracker Jack box. Do me a favor and look up Nancy Lemon when you get a chance."

"I—"

The woman held up her hand, cutting Evie off, and stepped into the back room.

Evie started to go after her, but she heard Fred call out, "Hey, Nancy. Long time no see. We keep missing each other."

Whatever Nancy said, Evie didn't catch it as another customer strolled in looking for his suit. She hurriedly retrieved it for him and was just about to dash into the back to apologize again when Fred appeared from the back room with his arms crossed and a scowl on his face.

Evie swallowed. This wasn't going to end well.

"Is it true you left fashion advice in the pockets of Miss Lemon's garments, Evie?" His tone was low and full of disappointment.

"Yes, but—"

He held up his hand in much the same way Nancy had just a few moments ago. "Have you been doing this to all of my clients?"

"Not to... *for*," Evie stressed. "And not all of them. Just the ones who could use a few pointers."

Fred ground his teeth together, making a muscle in his jaw pulse.

"It's her or me, Fred," Miss Nancy said. "I won't have some young fool telling me my creations aren't flattering."

Warning lights went off in Evie's head. *Creations? Nancy Lemon?*

"Oh, no," Evie said out loud, clutching at her chest. "Lemon Fashions? Home of the perfect cropped pants and the best darn bra a girl can buy? *That Nancy Lemon?*"

Miss Nancy beamed. "I did design the perfect bra."

"Ohmigod!" Evie squealed, pulling her shirt up to expose the red satin number that gave her the perfect amount of support and showed off her impressive cleavage. Made more impressive with the magical bra. "You are my favorite person in the entire world, Miss Nancy. A perfect genius if you ask me," she gushed. "I'm a huge fan of my cropped Lemons. I have three pair."

"So, you like my sportswear line, but not my runway. Interesting." She cast a glance at Fred. "A designer with less confidence could really get messed up with her advice. Better do something to nip this in the bud, or I'm finding a new dry cleaner come next week. Your choice."

"It's no contest," Fred said, still glaring at Evie. "This is the final straw, Evie."

"But—" Evie started.

"You're fired, Evie. Go home." Fred took Miss Nancy by the arm and escorted her out the door while Evie blinked, wondering how she'd ended up giving advice to a famous fashion designer. "I was only trying to help," she said again to herself as she grabbed her handbag and the McQueen dress from the back room and left with her head held high.

3

The door that separated the upstairs offices of Two to Mango from the stairwell to the restaurant below shut with a heavy thud from its hurricane-proof sturdiness as Lindy left Dora alone with Steve Franklin. The man's dark eyes were black with his anger, and Dora was nearly shaking in her shoes as he asked, "Did you find what you were looking for in Marco's office?"

Dora shook her head as she looked down at a pen on her desk. She was a terrible liar and she knew it.

"You did!" Steve cried out, and Dora jumped when he slapped his hands onto her desk and leaned over it toward her. "You little sneak," he growled out.

Dora had witnessed Steve laying into waitstaff who'd made him unhappy before, but she had never seen him this angry. It was looking more and more like he knew exactly what she'd found on Marco's computer, and that made him dangerous. She stepped back from the desk, eyeing the door with the hope she could escape. "I didn't find anything. I swear."

"How did you get into his computer?"

"I didn't!" Dora cried out as she backed up against the wall with the intention of sliding along it until she got to the door.

Steve stepped in her way, but instinct kicked in and Dora bolted around him toward the exit. She wasn't fast enough, though, and Steve grabbed her arm and yanked her back against his body, wrapping an arm around her waist. She gasped when a hard object was jabbed into her side, and she glanced down to see Steve was holding a gun.

The urge to cry was strong as Dora began to whimper. Flashes of her life's dreams played in her head: a handsome groom putting a ring on her finger; her imaginary children on swings; and Evie laughing as they frolicked in the waves as old women.

"Please, I don't know anything. I—" She inhaled sharply with pain when Steve dug the gun further into her side.

"I bet you know plenty, and that's too much for a smart girl like you."

He's going to kill me, she thought. Dora was as conflict averse as a person could be. She would rather eat an overcooked steak than send it back. She'd let someone cut in front of her in line instead of standing her ground. And she was the type to hand her purse to a potential mugger before he had the chance to snatch it. So what she did next shocked her as much as it shocked Steve.

Dora stomped her foot on top of his with all the strength she could muster and twisted in his arm to release herself as he reacted to the pain. She lifted her knee toward his groin and connected. Hard. Steve let out a groan of pain as he doubled over, and Dora grabbed the barrel of his gun.

For a split second, she felt the hard metal of the weapon in her fingers before Steve realized what she'd done. He pulled back, but she wasn't going to die without a fight. Somewhere deep down inside of herself, Dora found the strength to grab on to the pistol with her other hand and push it toward the ceiling while she held on tight. She stumbled forward and into Steve's chest as he pulled harder.

The gun exploded with searing heat that singed Dora's blouse as a loud bang made her ears ring. Then a deafening silence settled around her as time nearly stood still. *I'm dying*, Dora thought as she sank to her knees with the weight of Steve pulling her down with him, clutching at her as if she were his life preserver. She watched his face as he opened his mouth and blood bubbled out of it.

When it spilled over onto her chest she stared in horror as reality slapped her in the face. Dora wasn't the one dying. When Steve's eyes went blank, she didn't need to check to know what she'd done. *She'd killed Steve!*

Even though the third floor had been soundproofed to keep the restaurant noise from interfering with work in the offices, Dora couldn't be certain the sound of the gun hadn't been heard somewhere below. Marco Franklin was not the kind of guy to listen to excuses before acting, and if he found his father lying on the floor in a pool of blood while Dora was still there, she really would be dead. She needed to get out of there. *Fast.*

People say you never know how you're going to react in an emergency situation, but anyone who knew Dora would have bet money she was the type of woman who would freeze. They would have lost that bet, though, because she hopped up and sprang into action.

She grabbed the extra outfit she kept hanging behind her door. Without giving it a second thought, she quickly stripped out of her bloodstained clothes and into a travel-friendly shift dress and another pair of flats. Gathering her discarded clothes, she rolled them into a ball and shoved them into the tote bag she carried every day before she left her office.

She jogged down the stairs and exited the building still on

autopilot, and it wasn't until she was behind the wheel of her Toyota sedan that she began to shake. Dora knew she was in shock, but the fear that an entire restaurant had heard a gun go off and that Steve's body might have been found by now was a powerful motivator, and it kept the adrenaline rushing through her veins long enough for her to drive home.

When she got inside her rental, locked the doors, and closed all the blinds, Dora allowed herself to fall apart. She went to her kitchen in search of the bottle of wine she kept in the fridge but didn't manage to open the door. Instead she turned her back to it, leaned on the cold metal surface, and slithered down to the floor as her sobs finally escaped.

4

Dora wasn't sure how long she cried, but her burning eyes and mucus dripping from her nose finally forced her need for cleanliness to kick into gear. She got up from the kitchen floor in search of a tissue and began to process what she'd done. The financial information she'd uncovered definitely pointed to a money laundering scheme which she now knew both Steve and Marco were involved in. And considering Steve had jammed a gun in her side, she was pretty sure he would have killed her if she hadn't—

Dora's stomach clenched hard, and she barely made it to the bathroom to vomit up the entire contents. The tile floor was cold under her knees as she sat back and tried to think of what she should do. Lindy knew Dora had been in the office with an angry Steve just moments before the gunshot. And it wouldn't take a genius to know Dora was there when it happened. She had to turn herself in.

But she'd fled the scene, and anyone who had been raised on TV knew that was a darn good sign of guilt. Even worse, she was Two to Mango's accountant. When the truth came out about the money laundering scheme, who would ever believe she didn't know about it?

She chuckled dryly to herself as she stood up to brush her teeth. She'd underestimated Marco as a man who was so concerned with appearances that he didn't have brainpower to devote to his business. Apparently, he was far cleverer than she'd imagined, because he'd managed to run his scheme right under her nose.

Even though she looked guilty, Dora knew in her heart she had to go to the police.

Hello! The police, Dora thought as she hit her forehead with the palm of her hand. Dora's next-door neighbor, Brian, was a policeman. Even though he was almost two decades older than she, they'd become good friends over the years. They collected each other's mail when one went away, had shared a vegetable garden one year until they'd both realized neither had a green thumb, and even exchanged romance-gone-wrong stories over a few beers more than once. Brian was a man Dora could trust.

She grimaced as her empty stomach rolled again when she had to dig past her blood-soaked clothing to find her phone, and she called Brian to ask for his help.

It was less than a minute before Brian let himself in through her back door with a bottle of her favorite wine his hand. The moment Dora saw him she burst into tears, and he opened up his arms to her. "I don't know what's going on, but you just cry as long as you need to before saying a word."

Dora wanted to let the kind man's embrace comfort her, but the truth was that wasn't going to happen any time soon. Since she didn't have many tears left, she managed to control herself after a few moments and stepped out of Brian's embrace to whisper, "I killed someone."

His eyes widened slightly before he said, "Damn. This calls for whiskey." He walked into her kitchen, put the wine down on the counter, and reached into the cabinet over the fridge for the hard stuff.

"Brian?" Dora asked in disbelief at his calm reaction. "Did you hear what I said?"

Two glasses thumped onto the counter as he retrieved them. "You think you killed someone."

"Not *think*. I did!"

Brian gestured for Dora to take a seat at the kitchen table and handed her a glass of amber liquid. "Drink this and then you can tell me what happened."

The whiskey sloshed in her glass as Dora raised a shaky hand to take a sip, and after a hefty amount of alcohol burned its way down her throat, she relayed the entire story to him.

When she was done Brian got up and opened up the drawer where she kept plastic bags and pulled one out. He put it over his hand like a glove and grabbed her tote bag. "These the clothes?"

She nodded.

He rummaged through the bag as he said, "I'll take care of them, but Dora, you need to listen very carefully to me."

Brian's serious tone scared her, and Dora said, "Okay."

"I want you to pack a bag, and I'll drop you at Evie's house to hide. If the police come looking for you, do not let them know you're there."

"I don't understand. Why would I hide from the police?"

Brian let out a sigh with a pained expression. "The force is full of corruption right now, and from what you've told me, I'm worried the Franklin scheme might be bigger than we know. You're going to hide out at Evie's until the thumb drive arrives. Call me the minute it does, and I'll get you to a safe house. I'm going over to the restaurant to get the security tape footage that will prove your innocence. I don't trust it will get into the right hands, and I want to make sure what really happened doesn't get erased."

Dora's heart stopped when it occurred to her the tape wasn't the only thing Marco would want to erase. She picked up her glass of whiskey and downed the contents. Tears burned in her eyes, but they weren't from the drink. Dora had a sinking feeling that life as she knew it was going to be forever changed.

"Dora!" Evie called as she heard her best friend open the front door of her cottage and close it again. She carefully set the margarita glasses out, and added, "I hope you brought the big bottle of tequila. It's been one heck of a day."

Footsteps sounded on the tile floor of Evie's small cottage as Dora made her way through the house.

"You won't *believe* what happened," Evie continued as she dumped a generous helping of tequila into a shaker. "You know who Nancy Lemon is, right? Lemon Fashions? Anyway, she came in today and was *not* pleased with my unsolicited advice, and—" Evie, who'd just turned around and spotted a white-faced Dora, stopped mid-sentence, her insides turning cold with trepidation. Dora was the steadiest person she knew. Her best friend never let anything get to her, but in that moment, Dora looked like she'd just seen a ghost. "What happened?"

One lone tear rolled down Dora's face, and her bottom lip quivered as she whispered, "It's Steve... he... I..." She squeezed her eyes shut and shook her head.

"What?" Evie blinked at Dora, her ire up. "What did that jackhole do to you? Please tell me you kicked him in the nads. Did he get handsy?" Steve had always given Evie the creeps.

Dora slowly shook her head, her mouth working but no words escaping her lips. The faint *tap, tap, tap* of dog nails on the tile filled the silence as Sunshine, Evie's dog, trotted into the room. The little bichon ran up to Dora and jumped on her leg, desperate for attention. Dora glanced down at the little dog for just a moment and snapped out of her horrified trance. But instead of picking up the dog as she usually would, she ran over to the kitchen window and quickly lowered the blinds. "Help me close all of the blinds, Evie," she ordered as she ran to the dining room and started yanking on the cord to lower the blinds on the French doors. "I can't be seen here. It's too dangerous for both of us."

"Whoa, Dora. Come on. Don't you think you're overreacting just a little?" But even as she asked the question, she helped Dora get the windows covered. If it was important to Dora to sit in the dark after whatever happened with her boss, Evie was down for it. She'd do whatever Dora needed. Ride or die. Dora and Evie were besties for life.

Dora paused before disappearing into the living room and turned sad eyes on Evie. "I wish I was, honey. But I..." The words got caught in her throat and she just shook her head and hurried into the other room.

Not sure what else to do, Evie ran into her bedroom, where the blinds were already closed, and grabbed a handful of candles out of the drawer that housed all of her date-night supplies. After searching through a handful of condoms, lube, and silk ties, she finally found the lighter that was hiding in the back. A small smile played on her lips as she recalled the month before when her on-again, off-again boyfriend Trace had gotten really creative with the red silk and melted caramel. Who knew that caramel was better than candle wax?

"Evie?" Dora's frantic voice called from the other room. "I think someone's watching the house."

Evie slammed the drawer shut and ran into the other room to find Dora peeking out through the blinds, one hand pressed to her throat. "What do you mean someone is watching the house? Why would they do that? Because you kneed your boss where the sun don't shine? Wait. Knowing him it might have considering he went to—"

"Evie! I didn't knee him, I *killed* him. And now people are looking for me." Dora's eyes were wild, and she turned a putrid shade of green.

The candles landed with a thud on the coffee table where Evie dropped them, followed up by a softer thud when one rolled off and hit the floor. Her eyes went wide as her friend's words started to sink in. "You did what? You can't be serious."

Another tear rolled down Dora's cheek as she just nodded and turned her attention to the window again. Her shoulders sagged as she let out a heavy sigh. "Oh, thank goodness. I think the person outside is your neighbor. He just disappeared into his house."

Evie blinked at her, trying to keep up. "Long black hair? Tattoos covering both arms? Hotter than Trace's spicy martini? I swear if I wasn't already dating a rock star—"

"That's him." Dora sank into the couch and sucked in deep breaths.

Evie shoved some candles aside and sat on the coffee table in front of Dora, leaning down to pick up Sunshine. She needed the soft pooch to settle her rattled nerves. She looked her best friend in the eye and said, "Tell me everything."

Dora stared at the little dog and started to talk. She filled Evie in on how she'd broken into Marco's computer, uncovered a money laundering scheme, and how she'd been confronted and threatened by Steve. "That's when he pulled his gun on me."

Evie let out a gasp. "No!"

"Yes." Dora took Sunshine out of Evie's hands and cuddled the dog tight to her chest. "We fought. The gun went off. He's dead, and I was too scared Marco would come up and I'd be next, so I just left him there."

"It's self-defense then." With her heart pounding against her ribcage, Evie jumped up and ran to grab her phone. "You have to tell the police, Dora. If you don't, you're going to end up in an orange jumpsuit. And we both know orange is soooo not your color." A shudder rolled through her as she imagined Dora locked up in a maximum security prison with women named Cue Ball and Pinkie Pearl as cellmates. Dora couldn't kill a fly; she'd never survive life in the big house. "We'll call them now and explain everything. Surely they have security cameras that will show what really happened."

Dora popped up off the couch and yanked the phone away from Evie. "I already talked to Brian. He said to lay low until tomorrow. He went to get the tapes."

"Why?" Evie frowned. "Don't they want your statement? And if Brian knows, then why are all my blinds drawn?"

"Evie," Dora said in a hushed whisper. "He said there is corruption at the Pensacola police station, and he doesn't know who we can trust. So I'm to hang out here and lay low."

"Corruption?" Evie placed her hands on her hips and shook her head. "I always did think Leonard Kemp was on the take. Did I ever tell you about the time he tried to get me to polish his knob in exchange for not giving me an indecent exposure citation?" She shuddered again. "Old pervy bastard. He's over seventy years old."

"He wanted you to wax his vintage T-bird, Evie," Dora said, rolling her eyes.

"No, he didn't. I specifically remember him leaning against his red—oh. T-bird." She tsked, secretly pleased that she'd seemed to calm her friend down enough to at least correct her on the indecent exposure story. "Well, I still think it was a euphemism."

Dora moved toward the window again, no doubt to peer out at the street, but before she got there, someone knocked on the front door once and then barged right in, the door banging open. Dora flung herself against the wall, flatting herself to the sheetrock.

"Hey, baby," Trace, Evie's long and lean rocker and sometimes boyfriend, called as he kicked the door shut. "I'm back! Ready for another hot night of caramel and orga—"

"Dora's here!" Evie said brightly, waving at her friend behind him. Her heart swelled as she stared at Trace's perfect backside. It had been more than three weeks since she'd seen him last. He was a bass player in a local band, and they were on the road a lot. It wasn't unusual for him to surprise her when he rolled back into town.

Trace turned his brilliant blue eyes on Dora and gave her an easy smile. "Ahh, hey, Dora. Didn't know you were going to be here."

"It's margarita Tuesday." Dora blew out a breath and slid down the wall.

Trace's eyebrows rose as he turned back to Evie. "Isn't today Thursday?"

"We both needed to blow off some steam." She linked her arm through his and pulled him into the kitchen. Once they had a bit of privacy, Trace pulled Evie into his arms and gave her a searing kiss that made her tingle all the way down to her toes.

"Missed you, babe," he muttered against her lips.

Man, her rocker was yummy, but now wasn't the time. Evie pressed a hand to his chest and gently pushed him back. "Me, too. But it's not going to happen. Dora needs me tonight."

Disappointment flashed in his soulful eyes, but he quickly switched gears and gave her a lopsided grin. "So, no caramel?"

"It doesn't look good. Sorry." She chuckled as Sunshine ran

into the kitchen and started yapping at Trace. "Looks like Sunshine's a little jealous."

Trace reached down and pulled the bichon into his arms. "How are you doing, Sushi?" he asked the dog as she licked his face.

"Her name is *Sunshine*," Evie said, just as she always did when he called her dog Sushi.

"Come on, Evie. She looks like a little ball of rice." His voice changed to the universal baby-talk tone nearly everyone used for pets. "I could just eat you up in one bite!" He pressed his lips to Sunshine's head and gave her a kiss. Then he grinned at Evie.

She shook her head at him, wondering what all his bandmates would think. But then she remembered the redwood tree-sized drummer who talked that way to Sush—*Sunshine!*—when he'd met her too. "Whatever. But if she stops responding to her actual name, you're the one who is taking her to obedience school."

"Just roll with Sushi and everything will be fine," Trace said, winking at her.

Evie took Sunshine from his arms and tucked her against her chest. "Okay, rock star. Time to go. It's girls' night, and we have margaritas to drink."

Trace gave her a remorseful look. "You're sure?"

"I'm sure. Dora's having a bad day."

He nodded. "All right. Call me tomorrow?"

She set Sunshine on the floor and then pressed up onto her tiptoes and gave him a quick kiss.

He pulled her in and deepened the kiss, making it clear he wasn't thrilled about leaving. She wasn't either to be honest. Trace was one heck of a good time, and it had been *weeks*. But Dora was her bestie and she needed her.

"It's margarita time," she said, pulling back.

"I could be one of the girls," he teased even as he let her lead him toward the front door.

"Trust me when I say that's entirely untrue." Evie swept her gaze down his body, letting her attention linger just below the belt.

He laughed. "Night, Dora. Watch her as she mixes the margaritas. She's been known to be heavy-handed on the tequila."

"I need it," Dora muttered. Then her head snapped up. "You never saw me here, right, Trace?"

"Uh..."

"Dora doesn't want anyone to know she's here," Evie said quickly. "She's laying low for a bit. Just don't say anything if anyone asks where I am." If someone was looking for Dora, no doubt they'd check at Evie's house, but there was no need to broadcast her whereabouts. And if they did look for her at the little beach cottage, all of the blinds were closed, and the lights would be out. It would look like no one was home.

"Sure thing." He mimed tipping a hat and disappeared out the front door.

"Come on," Evie said, pulling her friend to her feet. "First we'll get the margaritas. Then I'll read your palm, and we'll finish with Bridget Jones. She always makes you feel better."

Dora blotted her eyes and sniffed. "She is a hot mess."

"The best kind." Evie tugged her friend into the kitchen and pressed a margarita into her hand. "Drink up. We have a lot to get through tonight."

But what Evie really meant was that Dora had a lot to set aside for the night. If they could just make it through to the next day, and Brian managed to clear Dora of any wrong doing, then she was sure her friend would be all right. Until then, Evie had work to do.

5

D ora sat at Evie's table and glanced at her watch for what seemed like the hundredth time. It was early afternoon, almost a full forty-eight hours after the *incident*—as Evie had taken to calling it—at work. Dora had spent the entire previous day waiting for Evie's mailman to show up with the flash drive, only to have him skip them due to no mail. She's been tormented when she realized she had to wait another whole day. "What time did you say your mail carrier usually gets here?"

Evie sighed and focused on the nail she was filing. "Would you relax? He'll get here when he gets here. Billy is the best."

"You're just saying that because he has a crush on you," Dora said, tapping her fingertips on the table while trying to be careful to not smudge her freshly painted nails. She wasn't usually the fidgeting type, but that afternoon she was ready to jump out of her skin.

Evie shrugged. "No, I'm not. He won me over when he saved Sunshine from Mrs. Pickett. She's a speed demon on her motorized wheelchair, and she was trying to scoop up Sunshine to take her to her lair. She kept talking about dressing her up in princess outfits and letting her granddaughter roll her around in a stroller just for their entertainment. Can you imagine Sunshine enduring that nonsense?"

Dora glanced at the pup in question. Sunshine stared up at Evie, her amber eyes sullen and then covered her face with a paw as if to say, *No, Mom, I can't imagine that.*

"I know, sweetie," Evie said to Sunshine and chuckled. "I'd never let that happen to you. And thanks to Billy for saving you from that horrible fate." She glanced at Dora. "Sunshine is just like my first boyfriend. She hates clothes."

"I remember," Dora said, recalling the numerous times Danny stripped at the beach to go skinny dipping even when no one cared to join him. "Speaking of boyfriends, what's going on with you and Trace?"

"What do you mean?" Evie asked.

"How's it going?" Dora asked, mostly to just distract herself from her own troubles.

"Fine. You saw him last night. Didn't we look like we're good?" She moved her file to another nail.

"Sure. But when is he gonna get around to putting a ring on it? You two have been dating for what? Two, three years?"

Evie sucked in a breath and gave Dora a warning glance. "Two and a half, but he's gone a lot. Neither of us are worried about making anything legal."

"Right. Because then you'd have to make a commitment. Can't have that," Dora said in a slightly teasing voice. Evie pretended to be all free love and no commitments, but she knew her friend was head over heels in love with her bass player. And he was just as gone for the free spirit who was so commitment-phobic she couldn't even hold a job for more than six months. Honestly, Dora wasn't even worried that Evie had lost her job at the dry cleaner. It was just about time for her to make the switch anyway. "You're gonna lose him one of these days, Evie. You know he wants to marry you."

"No one needs a piece of paper, Dora," she said, frowning. "I'm here and not going anywhere. Why do I need to legally bind myself to another person? That's so... eighteenth century."

"Oh, Evie. You know I love you, right?"

The other woman nodded but averted her eyes, obviously aware a *but* was coming.

Dora reached out and grabbed Evie's hand. "You're just scared. Not only is he the best thing that's ever happened to you, he also adores you, E. You should probably try to get over that before he gets tired of waiting."

"You're the best thing that's ever happened to me," Evie said, holding her friend's gaze.

Dora's heart swelled. "I love you, too, but I'm not going to be warming your bed anytime soon."

"Anyway..." Evie checked her nails and nodded as if she were satisfied. Then she grabbed Dora's hand and tsked. "Look what you did to your nails already."

"Darn it." Dora glanced down at her right hand and winced when she saw she'd smudged two of her freshly painted nails. Even though no one had shown up at Evie's looking for her, Dora was still really jumpy. It was just a matter of time before someone realized she'd killed Steve, right?

Evie soaked a cotton ball with nail polish remover and got to work, redoing Dora's messed-up manicure. "After this, it's pedicure time."

Dora curled her toes and shook her head. "You know I don't like it when anyone touches my feet."

Evie gave her an are-you-kidding-me look. "Please. The last time I got my magic hands on your toes there was a lot of moaning and sighing."

Even Dora had to admit that Evie was the best at mani-pedis.

One of her many, many jobs included working at a local nail bar. "Fine. Just don't tickle my arches. That drives me crazy."

"I'll do my best." Evie finished up Dora's two smudged fingers and then admired her handiwork. "I do rock at the French tips, don't I?"

"You do." Dora sat back and tried to not touch anything. As much as she liked mani-pedis, she never managed to sit still long enough for the polish to dry. There was an eight in ten chance that she'd smear at least one more nail before they were done.

"Let's do your toes in the living room. It will be comfier," Evie said, getting up from the table.

Dora didn't argue. She got up, and with Sunshine at her heels she moved to the other room and sat on the couch. The dog jumped up and settled into her lap. As Dora petted the little dog, she started to feel as if the day before had been some sort of dream. Like it wasn't real. She hadn't really killed someone, had she? It was surreal to be in the house Evie inherited from her grandmother, letting Evie pamper her, while Steve was dead and not one police officer had come looking for her. Not even Brian.

Steve had died in Dora's office. Dora had spent the morning glued to the local news channels, waiting for the news of the local restaurateur's death to be announced. But there was nothing. Not even a passing mention. How had the media missed his death? Surely he'd been taken to the local morgue. Someone had to have heard the dispatch when the call came in, right? So why wasn't there any reporting, and why wasn't anyone looking for his killer? And where was Marco? Even if the police were keeping this under wraps, Marco would be out for blood.

None of it made sense to Dora, but then she wasn't law enforcement. She had no real idea of how things worked in actual police investigations, only what she'd seen on television.

"Okay!" Evie called, appearing in the living room with a

plastic tub of water. "Soak your feet. I'm going to go grab my paraffin supplies."

"You don't have to do all of that," Dora said, glancing at the door. What if Marco barged in while her feet were wrapped in plastic booties and hot wax? She'd probably slip and hit her head on the coffee table as she tried to get away.

"Yes, I do. Who knows how long it's been since you had those feet pampered? I bet it was last fall, right? You dodged me the last few times I asked you to join me at the day spa."

Dora winced. Evie had a point. But what difference did it make if she had soft feet if she was just going to wind up in jail? Her face must've given her thoughts away because Evie pointed a finger at her and in a stern voice said, "Don't you even go there, Dora Winslow. This was self-defense, and Brian is going to make sure this goes away. If he doesn't, I will."

The look on Evie's face was so fierce and full of determination that Dora cracked the tiniest of smiles for the first time all day. Her friend really would go to the end of the earth for her. "Ride or die, right?"

"Thelma and Louise until the end," Evie said with a sharp nod.

"Okay. Well, if we're going to possibly be on the run, I might as well have pretty toes for the journey," Dora said.

"That's my girl." Evie beamed at her and got to work.

6

Dora looked at Evie, who sat back on the couch with her feet propped up on the coffee table, showing off her new pedicure and sipping champagne. Evie asked her, "Are you sure you don't want any of this? It's delicious."

Dora, who was sitting next to her, was still sporting cheap flip flops as her toenails dried. She pressed a hand to her stomach and shook her head. "My stomach is in knots. Do you have any ginger ale?"

Evie waved a hand. Dora liked to switch to ginger ale any time she got too tipsy for her liking, and Evie kept it on hand for her friend. "It's in the fridge." She sent Dora a side-eye glance. "I've got vodka too. A little of that in your drink wouldn't hurt, right?"

"Gah! No. I'll just get the ginger ale." Dora stood and started to stride toward the kitchen.

"Careful of the toes!" Evie called after her.

"Right." Dora stiffened, aware that her ability to girl had left the building a while ago, and she started to waddle like a penguin, careful to preserve her pedicure.

Evie snickered. As Dora riffled through the fridge for the soda, Evie must have peaked through the blinds and spotted the mail truck a few houses down, because she cried out, "Dora! Billy's almost here."

"He is?" Dora ran out of the kitchen with a ginger ale bottle in her hand. "Finally!"

The two women watched as Billy made his way to her neighbor's house and then turned in the direction of Evie's cottage. Evie automatically opened the door, already waving, when Dora spotted a solid white van speeding down the street straight toward Billy.

"What the hell?" Dora asked over Evie's shoulder.

"Billy, look out!" Evie called, desperately waving for him to get out of the way.

In a blur of white, Sunshine darted out of the house, headed straight toward Billy.

"No! Sunshine, come back!" Evie rushed out of the house after her pup.

Dora panicked and yelled, "Evie! No!" But Evie didn't slow down. She was too focused on the dog running toward the street to see the real danger.

Dora wasn't though. She watched a stocky man wearing a ski mask jump from the back of the van and grab Billy. Ignoring the danger for herself, she began to run toward Billy and yelled, "Get your hands off him!"

Another man with huge arms covered in tattoos jumped out of the van as the first guy held Billy by his blue button-down postal uniform shirt. He sneered as he yanked on the mail bag.

"No!" Dora cried as the tattooed guy succeeded in ripping the mail bag from Billy's grasp and took off at a dead run.

His conspirator released Billy and rushed for the van, too.

"Let go, you two-bit thief," Billy shouted, as he ran after

them, his fist held high in the air. "Neither snow, nor rain, nor heat, nor a bunch of crooks will stop me!"

"Wow," Dora said as she stopped next to Evie, who had Sunshine safely in her arms, to watch Billy. The mailman was actually gaining on the van. "That guy takes his job seriously."

When Billy reached the white van, he jumped on the back. The driver slammed on the brakes, and both Dora and Evie let out a gasp when the tattooed thief hopped out of the sliding van door, grabbed Billy, and tossed him into the vehicle like he was a sack of potatoes.

"No!" Dora cried again, and for the second time in two days she surprised herself by not cowering in fear. She took action. Her cheap sandals lived up to their name as they flip-flopped over the pavement while she ran to the mail truck with Evie hot on her tail. They both tried to jump into the driver's seat, but Dora had gotten there first and yelled, "Calling it!"

"Dammit," Evie said, conceding to their lifelong rule for who had rights to pretty much anything they both wanted.

Dora slammed the truck into gear as Evie and Sunshine barely managed to get in, and Dora gunned it with the hope of catching the getaway van that contained Evie's treasure of a mailman, the mailman's precious mailbag, and very importantly to Dora, the package with the flash drive that had proof of Marco's crimes.

Unfortunately, mail trucks don't have V-8 engines. Speed is not their most important feature, and the van already had a head start. But Dora gave it her all. She didn't even slow down to take the upcoming left turn.

As she yanked the wheel to the left, packages flew to the right with enough force the mail truck teetered a bit on two wheels before slamming back down on all four, engaging the two previously spinning wheels to give them a jolt forward.

"To the right!" Evie yelled once she could be heard over the wheel-screeching results of Dora's precarious turn. Not that it stopped her from performing the stunt another time. But it only took one more street before the van was no longer in sight. And when they got to the T intersection, it was clear they'd lost the bad guys, Billy, and the package with the flash drive.

Dora slapped her hands down on the steering wheel in frustration, and Evie wailed, "Poor Billy! We have to call the police."

"No," Dora said sternly as she pulled the mail truck over to the side of the road. "Let me call Brian." She lifted her hip to dig her phone out of her back pocket, a little surprised it was still there considering the wild ride and the state of the packages in the mail truck.

Brian picked up on the first ring. "Dora," he said, a little too breathless to sound casual.

But, Dora thought, *he's likely worried about me.* Her heart sank as the reality of what just happened hit her and she relayed the events to Brian. Without the flash drive, she didn't have any proof of the money laundering scheme, and she knew as well as any good accountant did that there were ways for Marco to cover his tracks. A whole new set of books and a few well-placed clues, and Dora would be on the hook for more than the accidental death of Steve Franklin. She asked, "What do I do now?"

"You're sure the kidnappers have the package?" Brian asked with a touch of optimism in his voice that made Dora uncomfortable.

Dora didn't have time to think that over at the moment because she was distracted by a woman's voice calling out, "Billy! Billy, I need your help!"

She looked out the window to see a woman wearing a cotton dress that had the shape of a flour sack. She also had big pink rollers in her hair as if she'd stepped off the set of a nineteen-sixties sitcom.

"I've got this," Evie said, and she got out of the truck to deal with the woman while Dora continued her conversation with Brian.

Dora said, "They've got Billy's mailbag which had to have had the package I sent to Evie with the flash drive since he was on his way to her front door." *Or was he,* she pondered as she recalled that Billy had hesitated for a moment before the bag was snatched.

"Good—I mean," Brian paused. "I mean at least they got what they wanted and you're no longer in danger."

"What?" Dora let out a noise of disbelief. "I *am* still in danger. You don't really believe Marco is just going to let this go now that he has the flash drive, do you? I—" She whispered the next words. "I accidentally killed his father."

"I know. I'm sorry. That came out wrong. I mean that at this very second you aren't in danger. And you *might* be fine." He let out a heavy sigh. "Look. Just lay low for a while, and I'll get this sorted out. Whatever you do, don't breathe a word of this to anyone. Got it?"

Dora frowned. Brian didn't seem very concerned about her wellbeing. His advice to lay low and not tell anyone about what she knew while she waited for him to do something was more suspicious than the milk in Evie's fridge. "And Billy?" she asked as she watched Evie take the hands of the woman in the housedress as if she was comforting her.

"He'll be fine. I've got this. Don't you worry about a thing."

Dora's stomach was in knots, and when her call with Brian ended, she stared at the phone in confusion. He had not acted like someone who was looking out for her best interests. The man had acted as if he was happy the robbers had gotten the package and brushed off her concerns about the kidnapped mailman. Something was definitely off.

7

"Dora!" Evie called. "We have a situation."

That's putting it mildly, Dora thought as she raised her eyebrows at her friend through the windshield of the mail truck.

"Miss Carol here has a problem we need to help solve," Evie said. Dora stepped out of the mail truck as Evie continued, "Mr. Whiskers is stuck." She pointed at a large, red maple tree with the kind of branches kids and cats loved to climb. Up near the top sat a tabby meowing in distress.

Dora looked at Miss Carol in disbelief. "You want us to climb up and get your cat?" She shook her head in dismissal. "The moment that cat is hungry he'll come down for food."

"No," the woman said with a shaky voice that made Dora think she was on the verge of tears. "No, he won't." Miss Carol's tone turned to indignation as she threw her shoulders back. "And Billy wouldn't have questioned me. He'd have climbed right up that tree and gotten Mr. Whiskers."

"She's right," Evie said. "And since we're—" Evie paused to search for the right words that wouldn't give away what was really going on. "Well, *because* we're *filling in* for Billy, it's our responsibility to help."

"You're serious?" Dora asked Evie even though she already knew the answer. Evie had a soft spot for animals that defied logic.

Evie put her hands on her hips and gave Dora *the look*. The one that said logic is not the answer to everything. And Dora knew that she wasn't going to win this one. Some fights weren't worth having. The least she could do to salvage the situation was make sure it was done right. She marched over toward the tree as forcefully as possible in flip flops with toe bridges curling up her tootsies, making her stride appear a bit like that of a duck.

Miss Carol whispered loudly enough to Evie that Dora overheard. "What's with your friend's choice of footwear?"

Dora hoisted herself up to the first branch of the tree, already regretting that she didn't make Evie do the climbing. She ground her teeth in anger at Miss Carol's judgment before she spat out, "Ingrown toenail. Okay?"

"She's a bit touchy, isn't she?" Miss Carol said, this time not bothering to whisper.

Before Dora could hop back out of the tree and tell Miss Carol to call the fire department, Evie answered. "She's saving your cat, Miss Carol. A little respect."

It was hard to stay mad at a friend who had her back, and Dora continued to climb up the tree to lure Mr. Whiskers from his perch. She had a great deal of respect for felines. It was hard not to appreciate a species that could wrap humans around their furry tails with a purr, yet only give affection when the mood struck. Truthfully, Dora wished she could be more like them. Especially when it came to men.

Dora chipped a nail on the rough bark of the tree and huffed in annoyance as she got closer to the cat. She thought about how cagey Brian had been on the phone call, and while she'd need to talk it over with Evie, she had the gut instinct her neighbor was just like most men in her life... not to be trusted.

Dora had been burned by more than one man in her lifetime. She knew better than to trust them any further than her wimpy arms could throw one, and she was seriously starting to regret placing her life in Brian's hands.

"Meow!" Mr. Whiskers cried as Dora got close enough to reach for him. The cat didn't let her lift him from his perch though. Instead he hopped onto Dora's shoulder and dug his claws in.

"Ouch!" she cried out, sure the tabby had drawn blood.

"Don't you hurt him!" Miss Carol called from below.

Dora had a fleeting desire to fling the cat off her back and let him prove he could land on his feet while using up one of his lives. But she knew her anger wasn't for the cat. It was about the frustration she had over trusting another man who'd let her down.

When she got to the bottom of the tree and Mr. Whiskers dug into her flesh one more time to launch himself into his owner's arms, Dora's anger faded. The tears of joy on Miss Carol's face was reward enough for the good deed she done.

"Thank you for saving my baby!" Miss Carol cried. "I don't know how I'll ever thank you."

"You do make a mean shortbread cookie," Evie said. "Dora loves sweets."

"Then I'll be by later with a double batch." Miss Carol said before she snuggled into her cat and smothered him with kisses. And despite the bleeding welts on her shoulder, Dora smiled, satisfied with the job she'd done.

Dora's joy was short lived, though. The moment the two of them got back to the truck, where they found Sunshine sitting in the driver's seat keeping watch over the mail, Dora knew she had to tell Evie her suspicions about Brian. "We have to talk."

Dora started up the truck. As she began to drive, Sunshine jumped into her lap with a rubber-banded stack of mail in her mouth. Dora pushed at the dog with the back of her hand. "Evie, control your little beast. I'm trying to drive."

"Dora! Sunshine is telling you we need to deliver the mail."

"What?" She looked over at her friend. "Of all the—" Dora sighed, noting Evie was giving her that look again. "No. No. No. No," she chanted, aware it was a useless plea.

"You heard the man," Evie said. "Neither snow, nor rain, nor heat—"

"Or kidnapping. I get it." Dora shook her head as she pulled in close to a mailbox. She checked the address. Miraculously it was the correct one, and the mailbox door creaked as she tugged it open to deposit the bundle of mail Sunshine had dropped in her lap.

They drove slowly down the street with Sunshine scampering back to the pile of mail that had fallen off the shelves, magically retrieving the right bundle for each house.

"That dog is kind of freaking me out right now," Dora said as she double checked the bundle Evie had just given her.

"Right?" Evie said with a lilt at the end as if it was a question. "So, what did Brian say?"

"It's what he didn't say that has me worried, Evie." Dora pulled outgoing mail from a mailbox and handed the shoebox-size package to her friend before lowering the red flag. She snapped the door shut and turned to stare intently at Evie. "He was super cagey about the whole thing. He actually seemed happy the package was stolen. And—" She let out a sigh as the pain of yet another man betraying her made her heart ache. "He said I might not have anything to worry about. How much sense does that make? I killed a man!"

"It was self-defense!" Evie cried out, quick to defend her best friend.

"True," Dora agreed. "But there's no way Marco is going to let me off easily."

"You're right. So what do we do?"

Sunshine let out a yap and scampered back to the pile of mail. She grabbed a manila bubble mailer and brought it to Dora. Taking the package without inspecting it, Dora said, "This is going to sound crazy, but I'm afraid saving Billy is up to us."

"Oh boy. You really think we need to free him from the kidnappers?" Evie asked.

Sunshine scrambled into Dora's lap and pawed at her arm for attention. Dora ruffled the dog's head to satisfy her. "Do you trust Brian to do it after what I just told you?"

Sunshine barked and pawed at Dora again with more force. "Jeez," she said as she held the package in her hand out of the way and glared at the dog. "What is it with you tiny animals maiming me?"

"Dora!" Evie grabbed the package out of her hand. "Oh my god. Look!" She held it up so Dora could see who it was addressed to.

Dora recognized the neat script right away and gasped as she grabbed the envelope back out of Evie's hand. "The flash drive!"

"The robbers didn't get it! You know what this means?" Evie asked.

Dora nodded as she moved to tear the envelope open.

Evie snatched it back. "Don't you dare! That's addressed to me. Don't you know it's illegal to tamper with the mail?"

Dora glanced around the mail truck, looking at the piles of letters and packages strewn about before raising her eyebrows at her friend. They'd already crossed the line when it came to breaking postal laws.

Evie gave her a smirk and tore the package open. Then she

let out a squeal as she unfolded the tissue paper and held up the purple-and-turquoise silk scarf Dora had gotten her. "I love it!" She draped it around her neck as Dora reached for the flash drive that had fallen into Evie's lap and gripped it tightly in her palm. Evie leaned over and embraced Dora. "You're the best friend ever. I don't know how I'd ever live without you. Thank you."

Dora patted her friend on the back, but she didn't feel an ounce of the same joy Evie did. Not only was she in grave danger, she'd also managed to pull her best friend and an innocent mailman into the fray. The summer heat that had made her skin damp with sweat as they delivered the mail couldn't warm up her heart because the chill of the danger she and Evie faced was too cold to ignore.

8

Evie's concern over Dora's state of mind was multiplied when she noticed how pale her friend was, and she wondered if the beads of sweat on her brow were actually from the Pensacola heat. She supposed it was a natural reaction to the last forty-eight hours. Not only were they in danger from Marco Franklin and whoever he was involved with, but they now had to figure out how to save an innocent man. Tempted as she was to call the police and let them handle it, she was afraid Dora was right. Brian and other members of the police force were likely corrupt, and they had no idea who they could trust.

Evie reached for her friend's clenched hand to find her fingers were ice cold. "Honey." She tried to loosen the death grip Dora had on the flash drive. "I don't think it's safe to keep this on us. Do you?"

Dora shook her head. "Nothing is safe, Evie." She swallowed hard. "Marco and his goons are going to kill me. You. And Billy—"

Dora's phone vibrated in her pocket with a call, and she

pulled out her cell to see who it was. The moment she looked at it she let out a little scream and dropped her phone.

It clattered on the floor before Evie snatched it up. "Marco Franklin? Are you freaking kidding me? Does that lowlife think you're actually going to answer?"

"Maybe I should." Dora whined. "Maybe––"

"No."

"But––"

"Shhh," Evie said, determined to calm her friend. "C'mon now. There's nothing good that can come from talking to Marco." She opened up Dora's phone and clicked on the contact info for Marco so she could block his calls. "We're smart women. We can figure this out. We just need to hide this for a while until we know who we can trust. There has to be someone in law enforcement in this town who isn't dirty. The only question is where?"

"Don't ask me, Evie. Clearly, my judgement isn't to be trusted. You know how smart I am? I'm so smart I worked there for months before I saw Marco's money laundering scheme even though it was right in front of my eyes." Dora's voice raised an octave as she continued. "How the heck is someone like me supposed to stay alive when we can't even ask anyone for help?"

"Trusting people doesn't make you stupid. It makes you human." Evie tried again to get Dora to relax her fingers, and this time it worked. She lifted the small orange flash drive from Dora's palm and replaced it with Dora's phone. "We need a good hiding spot for this."

Sunshine let out a bark, and Evie glanced down to see the pup was leaning against Dora, offering comfort. Dora absent mindedly stroked the dog as Evie marveled at how clever her puppy was grabbing the right mail for each house as they made their way through the neighborhood delivering it.

Evie glanced down at the package in her lap and imagined what might be inside. Perhaps it was a present. And maybe it was for the woman's birthday the way Evie's package had been for hers. It made Evie imagine how happy some woman named Gertie Bonatelli would be when she received her gift. It really was amazing that you could send things all over the world right from your very own— "That's it! Dora, I know what to do with the flash drive."

She yanked the keys out of the mail truck's ignition and began to run the sharp edge of a key along the taped seam of the package in her lap.

"What are you doing?" Dora's tone turned sarcastic. "Tampering with the mail?"

"We're going to send Gertie here a little surprise. One that we're going to be there to get."

"What?"

The remaining tape popped when Evie tugged the box open and pulled out something wrapped in tissue. She removed the paper to reveal what appeared to be a Buddha statue, but a slot at the top of his head proved it was actually a piggy bank. "This is perfect!" She turned the bank over to remove the rubber stopper. A moment later, the flash drive clattered when she dropped it inside.

"Hold on," Dora said. She grabbed the bank and pulled the flash drive out to wrap it in tissue before putting it back inside the Buddha where it was now unable to move or rattle. She looked at Evie with a hint of smile. "I think this can work."

"Me too," Evie said, grinning at her. "See? We can totally do this."

Dora frowned. "Maybe we can. But we've got a mess to clean up before we head on over to New Orleans to pay Gertie a visit."

"We certainly do. First, we finish delivering the mail." This got a confirmation bark from Sunshine. "Who knew canines were so invested in the USPS? Do you think that's why they chase mailmen? I bet they have a sixth sense for it. Maybe they know the guy isn't doing his job right."

"Evie!"

Evie sighed. Dora had an annoying habit of pulling her out of her riffs, which was a shame because it was where she often found her best ideas. "Once we finish with the mail, we need to free Billy."

"Right," Dora said with renewed confidence that made Evie's shoulders fall in relief. "Does Billy have family?"

Evie shook her head, happy to have a competent Dora back. "He lives alone. His closest relatives are in Montana. Why?"

"Good. Since today is Saturday, that means once we deliver all the mail, we can return the truck to the post office."

Evie perked up. She'd had a quick stint as a mailwoman at one point a few years ago and understood how the system worked. "I know just where to drop off outgoing mail, so we're sure Gertie's package gets delivered, and then we have until Monday before anyone will know Billy's missing."

"By which time we should have set him free," Dora said.

Evie held up a hand for a high five. "We've so got this!"

Dora's palm smacked hers but then Dora frowned. "There's only one problem. We don't know where Billy is being held."

Evie said, "I bet it's at one of the businesses you found in Marco's files that they're using to launder the money. From what you said, they're all shady enough that a kidnapped man wouldn't draw much attention."

Dora narrowed her eyes at Evie. "You're a little too good at this. But I think you're right."

Evie grinned as she basked in the praise, and she decided to capitalize on her moment. "Do you want me to drive now?"

Dora snorted in her denial. "Fat chance." She took the keys

from Evie's hand and slid them back in the ignition before winking at Sunshine. "We'd better get moving. We've got mail to deliver."

Sunshine let out a happy bark before rushing over to the pile of mail to resume her job.

9

Dora rolled her eyes at Evie as she tugged on the short, plaid schoolgirl skirt Evie had insisted she put on. "I don't see how wearing this is going to help me blend in. I'm supposed to be your manager."

After Evie and Dora had delivered the mail and returned the truck and the outgoing mail, all while keeping up the ruse Billy was fine, they moved on to the next step of their plan. They were going to visit the strip club Marco was using as one of his money laundering venues in search of Billy. Evie suggested that cries of pain were awfully similar to those of passion and that maybe it would be easier to hide Billy that way. Since Dora had zero experience with strip clubs, she agreed to Evie's plan. Evie's reasoning sounded valid to her.

Evie said, "You're playing my manager because you've got a head for money. Wait..." She grinned. "There's a bad joke in there somewhere. Give me a minute."

"Evie!" Dora cried with impatience. "Just give me the knee socks." As she tugged them on, she mumbled, "If anyone dares to ask me to hit them one more time, they're going to see a meltdown that would make Britney proud."

"Damn. I'd like to see that, too," Evie said as she twisted in front of her full-length mirror to check out her backside. She was clad in a red sequin dress that barely covered her enough to be decent.

Dora studied her for a moment. "Do I want to know why you even own a dress like that?"

"Trace has a taste for—"

"Stop right there." Dora held her palm up. "I think I'd rather leave the reason up to my imagination."

"Suit yourself," Evie said before she smacked herself on the rump. "I swear I get hotter every year."

"Ugh." Dora took a look at her ridiculous get up and tugged the white button-down shirt that was tied at her midriff closer to the waistband of her skirt. "And I get fatter."

"What the heck are you talking about?" Evie asked. She was getting a little tired of Dora's constant drive toward perfection. Five pounds in either direction was nothing to be concerned about, yet her friend was a stickler for staying within a three-pound range to the point of near obsession. Although she supposed that had a lot to do with Dora's need for control and not so much about her self-worth. "You are so getting hit on when we go to that club, so hush up girl and let's get out of here."

Evie scooped Sunshine into her arms and started for the door.

"You're not bringing your dog, are you?" Dora asked, eyeing her as if she had two heads.

"I have to," Evie insisted, unwilling to leave her precious pup home alone. "What if Marco comes looking for you? If he only finds Sunshine, he might take his wrath out on her."

Dora went pale and swallowed.

"I'm sorry, honey!" Evie said quickly. "I didn't mean to freak you out. I'm sure I'm being paranoid. You know how I am about

Sunshine. She's just so precious and protective. I'm afraid I'd be worried about her the whole time. She can just ride along with us."

"All right," Dora said and took a deep, fortifying breath. "You're probably right. It's better if she's with us. Besides, she's our lucky charm. Without her, we might never have found the package in the mail truck."

"That's the spirit." Evie patted her pup's head and darted outside with Dora right behind her.

Once they got in Evie's car, reality set in. Getting dressed to go out was a fun thing that had made Evie forget the seriousness of what they were about to do. She'd enjoyed glamming Dora up to look more like a wild woman than the straightlaced accountant she normally was, but once they'd applied the last coat of lipstick, the harsh truth about what lay ahead fell over the two women like a lead blanket.

Sunshine sat in Evie's lap as her mistress pulled out of her driveway in the dark of night. Evie said, "Run over the plan one more time with me."

"Okay," Dora said. "We're going to go in and ask to talk to the owner, Dirk Jones. I'll say we're new to the area and I have a stable of girls he might be interested in. You are going to be the sample." She paused. "You do have panties on under that, right? Because what if he wants you to strip?"

"Relax," Evie said, even though she was far from following her own advice. "You know I've never been a modest person." To appease Dora, she added. "But don't worry. I have on panties and pasties."

"Pasties?" Dora let out a sigh. "Remind me why we picked the strip club to check out first?"

"Screams. And—"

"That was a rhetorical question." Dora sighed. "I'm sorry. Here you are being above and beyond the best friend in the world, on your thirtieth birthday no less, and I'm giving you a hard time about it. I'm just nervous."

Evie understood completely, and to lessen the tension, she asked, "Did you just say *hard* time? Because…" She waggled her eyebrows at Dora and got the intended effect when her friend laughed.

They drove in silence for a while, and Evie noticed Dora gazing out the window at the seedier section of Pensacola. It wasn't an area Evie frequented either, but she had a feeling Dora was a lot more uncomfortable than she was. "Hey," she said as she reached over and grabbed her best friend's hand. "There's nothing we can't get through. Think of all the things we've already survived."

Dora squeezed her fingers. "We have had a few adventures, haven't we?"

"It was definitely your turn," Evie said.

"Yeah? Well, this one's a doozy. You're welcome to bail at any time."

"Never," Evie said. "Remember our first day of kindergarten?" As if either of them could ever forget. That was the day Dora and Evie met. She recalled the way Dora had noticed Evie crying when her mother had left her in the classroom. She'd walked over, grabbed Evie's hand and said, "Don't cry. I'll be your friend." The two had been best friends ever since.

"I do."

10

E vie pulled into the parking lot of the strip club, and red light from the neon sign flashed over their heads as she parked in a spot under it. "Then you need to remember that we've stuck by each other through a whole lot. Remember bedazzled jeans?"

Dora nodded. "Crimped hair."

"Ugh," Evie said. "And denim everything."

"Oh my god, low rise jeans. Remember how you couldn't sit down without showing off your butt crack?"

"See?" Evie asked. "We've already survived flashing our coin slots. We can totally do this."

Dora laughed with her. "Okay. But next year? Let's just drink too many margaritas for your birthday. I'll even match you drink for drink and brave the hangover from hell."

"Oh man, you're daring me with tequila? Bring it, sister," Evie joked.

Dora blew out a breath and reached into her bra to hoist her breasts higher. "Bring it, I will." She gave Evie a serious look. "You remember what this guy looks like?"

Evie nodded. They'd found a picture of Dirk on the internet so they'd be able to spot him.

Dora smiled at Evie and said, "Good. Let's do this."

While Evie clutched Sunshine with one arm, the two women marched in time with each other toward the club entrance, their heels clicking on the pavement like a tribal beat. It occurred to Evie that Dora had agreed to their scheme a lot faster than usual, and she suspected it had everything to do with the danger she knew she was in. Danger Evie had every intention of helping Dora get out of unscathed. She'd meant it when she said she owed her best friend.

Nobody had ever believed in her the way Dora did. And nobody else had stuck with her through her many failures. Evie couldn't count the number of jobs she'd burned through, but what she did remember was that Dora had been there to help her pick up the pieces and move on every single time. She'd done the same for Evie when it came to her broken heart too.

So, when Dora pushed their way into the strip club, Evie was determined to do whatever it took to get Billy free and Dora one step closer to proving her innocence. *Anything.*

Dora took the lead, her shoulders back and her head held high, surprising Evie. She was exuding self-confidence and determination. *Good,* Evie thought, but an ache had formed in her gut. This wasn't exactly the nicest part of town, and Evie knew better than anyone that these weren't the type of people that cared to be messed with. They just needed to get the information they came for and then get the heck out of there.

"There he is." Dora paused and jerked her head toward a tall, dark-haired man at the end of the bar. "That's Dirk." She turned and glanced at Evie and Sunshine. "Give her to me. You can't audition with a dog in your arms."

Evie shook her head. "Not until after we talk to Dirk. It

wouldn't be professional for my manager to be carrying a small dog." Though Evie highly doubted Dirk Jones would give one flying fig about Sunshine. As long as Evie was willing to take it off, she was certain that was all he'd care about.

"Hey, gorgeous," a tall man with muscles that went on for days said to Dora, sliding up next to her and resting a hand on her hip. Dora stiffened, but before she could tell him to back off, he produced a one-hundred dollar bill and tucked it into her cleavage. "How about a lap dance before the rest of the punks in here wake up and notice you?"

Evie smirked as Dora pulled the bill out of her cleavage and held it out to the man. "I'm not a stripper." She waved to Evie. "I manage Candy over here, and right now we need to go talk to the boss man."

The Ken doll glanced over at the bar and frowned. "Jones appears to be busy." Then he glanced back at Dora. "It sure looks like you're dressed to shake that ass tonight."

"I—"

Evie grabbed the bill Dora was still holding and tucked it into her bra. "She'd love to. Dora, go give the man the dance he's asking for."

"What? No, I'm not—" Dora started.

"Give us just one sec," Evie said, smiling brightly at the man as she hooked her arm through Dora's and tugged her away a few feet.

"What are you thinking?" Dora hissed, keeping a wary eye on her admirer.

"I'm thinking we can use the money. Have you forgotten we're both out of jobs now? If we're careful, a hundred bucks will go a long way toward keeping the fridge full."

Dora closed her eyes and let out a barely audible groan.

Evie patted Sunshine's head as she added, "You know how to

shake it. Remember the moves we made up to Beyoncé's "Naughty Girl"?"

"Yes," Dora said, her tone hesitant.

"Just draw on those and you'll be great." Evie gave her a little shove. "I'll be right here if Ken doll gets handsy."

"A hundred bucks," Dora said under her breath as if she was trying to talk herself into it.

"You got this." Evie pulled her back over to the man and grinned. "Have fun. Sunshine and I will be right here watching." She leaned in closer to the man. "Remember, no touching."

"What if I pay extra?" he asked Evie.

She patted him on the shoulder. "Sorry man. That's against the rules. Take it or leave it."

He glanced at Dora again, his eyes glittering with anticipation. "All right. Let's do this, honey."

"This way," Dora said, boldly taking him by the hand and leading him over to an unoccupied chair.

"There she goes, Sunshine," Evie said to her pup. "Look at her. She's swaying her hips and flipping her hair like an expert. She even managed to flip her skirt just enough so that he got a peek of her backside."

Sunshine squirmed in her arms as if straining to see Dora.

"Oh, wow. She just gently pushed him down into the chair and straddled him, completely taking charge." Evie glanced down at Sunshine. "Can you believe that? I think our Dora might have missed her calling as a dominatrix. Who knew?"

Sunshine turned big brown eyes on Evie, giving her a look.

Evie laughed. "I know. You're right. She does have that no-nonsense attitude. If I didn't know her so well, I'd start to wonder if she had a collection of BDSM toys hiding in her closet."

A small crowd of business men moved, blocking Evie's view of Dora. But soon enough, Dora's head started to bob up and down in time to the slow beat of the music playing over the sound system. Evie giggled. She couldn't help it. Two days ago, the idea of Dora giving anyone a lap dance would've been the craziest thing she'd ever heard. That type of thing was definitely more Evie's scene. But after today, seeing her poor mailman get abducted and knowing what had happened back at Dora's office, this was nothing in comparison.

"Look at her sticking her butt out, Sunshine." Evie craned her neck, to get a better view. "And the way she's putting her rack right in his face without even touching him. Jeez. She's a freakin' natural."

Sunshine let out a small whimper and covered her eyes with a paw.

Evie shook her head. "Giving a good lap dance is nothing to be embarrassed about, Sunny. Workin' it with the right person can lead to a hot night in the bedroom."

"You know it," a stocky man said from right behind Evie just before his large hand landed on her barely clad butt cheek.

"Hey! Hands off the goods," Evie said, jumping back and putting plenty of space between them. "That's not how this works."

"You were the one who said good lap dances lead to something better. I was just giving you what you asked for, baby." He moved forward, his hand out as if he was going to grab her again.

Sunshine lifted her head and growled, baring her teeth.

"Whoa!" He took a few steps back and blinked as if he didn't quite believe what he was seeing. "Who let that prissy little beast in?"

"She's with me," Dora said, appearing right behind Evie.

"Gooood," the man said, drawing out the word and making Evie's skin crawl. "I always did like a two-for-one special."

Dora narrowed her eyes at the guy. "Back off, buddy, or I'm

going to let this sweet little dog go for her favorite body part."
She lowered her gaze, letting it linger just below the belt.

The man's face paled. And without saying another word, he
took off, disappearing into the crowd.

"Thanks," Evie said, grinning at her friend. "You have a
multitude of skills I didn't realize you possessed. Seriously, Dor,
that lap dance? It was pro level."

Dora frowned at her.

"Uh-oh. What happened? What'd he do?" Evie's ire rose, and
her entire body heated with irritation as she craned her neck
looking for the man who'd just been ogling Dora's assets.

"He gave me a tip." Dora produced a twenty but was still
frowning.

"Excellent." Relief rushed through Evie as she grabbed the
bill and shoved it into her bra with the hundred. "But why the
sourpuss face? Cash is good."

"Evie," Dora hissed. "You were supposed to be looking for
Billy, not watching me degrade myself for cash!"

Oops. Evie grimaced. Dora had a point. "All right. Sunshine
and I are on it. There's Dirk." She pointed to a tall guy with dark
hair who was standing near the door to the back room.

Dirk had his hand on a wall and was leaning over a girl in
glasses and a plaid skirt. She turned around and stuck her butt
out and he shoved money in her G-string, making her giggle as
she walked away.

"Hey, Dor-a." Evie sang out. "Looks like our friend Dirk has a
thing for the uptight librarian."

"Oh no." Dora shook her head. "I already took one for the
team. It's your turn. Remember the plan? You were going to
audition." She started to reach for Sunshine, but Evie took a step
back as she shook her head.

"Nope. My Jessica Rabbit look isn't going to work. You're

rocking what Dirk wants in a big way. Just give me three minutes. That's all I need to search the back." Evie gave her a bright smile. "Once you've enthralled him with your glorious cleavage, Sunshine and I will be quick like bunnies and find out if there's any sign of Billy.

Dora's jaw tightened. "I really hate you sometimes, you know that?"

"You love me." Evie winked at her. "Go on. As soon as you distract him with that great rack, Sunshine and I will get our search on."

Dora took a deep breath. And just like a pro, she strutted her way over to Dirk to put her assets to work.

Evie didn't hesitate. She weaved through the club and slipped through the door that led to the back. A dancer strode by, apparently unfazed by a new girl holding a small dog. She just nodded and waited in the wings for her turn on the stage.

Interesting, Evie thought. She'd expected to be questioned, but either the place had a lot of dancer turnover or no one cared enough to wonder what she was doing there. The place wasn't all that big. She poked her head into the three small offices. All of them were empty.

Unless the girls had Billy tied up in their dressing room, the place had turned out to be a dead end. Just to make sure, she pushed the door open to the dressing room and spied three women in various states of dress—or undress. No Billy. Before they could question her, she ran back into the club just as Dora shook her rump for the last time.

Dora's eyes locked on her friend's as Evie gave a tiny shake of her head. Evie watched as Dora stopped and said something to Dirk. He frowned after her as she hurried over to Evie. "Nothing?"

"Nothing." Evie scanned Dora's body with her gaze and

licked her lips dramatically. "Unless you want a new career. Looks like Dirk was interested."

"Oh my god," Dora hissed. "You are so not funny."

"Fine. Fine." Evie laughed as Dora shoved her out the door of the club.

11

"I'm not going in there like this," Dora insisted. It was one thing to strut around in stripper clothes in a strip bar, but she wasn't showing her face in Dildos R Us wearing an eleven-inch skirt that did almost nothing to cover her backside.

"But you'll wear a white button-down shirt that shows off your nips?" Evie said with a snicker.

"What?" Dora glanced down at her chest and groaned. "Those pasties would've really come in handy."

"Want mine?" Evie asked, already reaching into her shirt as if to peel them right off herself.

"No! Forget it." Dora felt her face go hot. She wasn't that desperate that she was going to share pasties with her bestie. "I'll just toss this sweatshirt on," she said, digging around in a duffle bag of workout clothes. "And these running tights."

"Suit yourself." Evie patted Sunshine's head, making no move to change her own outfit.

"I definitely will, thank you very much." Dora awkwardly changed in the passenger's seat, grateful it was dark out as she hastily shrugged out of the white shirt and tugged the sweatshirt on. After she'd switched her skirt for the workout pants, she looked down at her high heels and groaned. "These don't exactly go, do they?"

Evie giggled. "That's one way to class up your outfit."

Dora opened the car door and let out a heavy sigh. "Come on. At least I can use one as a weapon if we run into Marco or any of his minions."

"Now you're thinking." Evie followed her out of the car, but just as they got to the front door, she tugged on Dora's sleeve.

Dora glanced back at her, noting she was clutching Sunshine so tightly that the little dog had started to pant and squirm to get out of her mother's arm. "It's okay, Sunshine," Dora said, gently pulling her from Evie's grip. "She didn't mean to squeeze the stuffing out of you." She looked at her friend. "What's wrong?"

Evie ran a nervous hand through her hair. "It's just that I started to think about what you'd said about running into trouble. Do you really think Marco might be out looking for you at these places?"

Dora shrugged, trying to ignore the unease in her gut. "If Billy's here, there's a strong possibility, don't you think?"

"Right. Obviously. I guess I was just so caught up in our ruse at the strip club, I hadn't even thought about it." She bit her bottom lip and then reached into the tiny handbag she had slung across her shoulder. "He likely won't recognize me, but you..." She shoved a dark pair of sunglasses at Dora. "Put those on. With your hair and makeup all done up like that, the glasses will help."

Dora didn't see how wearing sunglasses, at night no less, along with workout gear and high heels, was going to do anything to help her maintain any sort of cover, but she put them on anyway. If she didn't, Evie was likely to have a meltdown right there in the seedy parking lot.

Evie blew out a breath. "Okay. Let's go find Billy."

Still clutching Sunshine, Dora held the door open for Evie

and followed her in. "Your turn to distract the cashier. I'll check out the back this time."

"Sure, Dora. But let's just take a look around the store first, let him eye the goods a bit before I dazzle him with my sparkling personality."

Considering a sex shop was more Evie's comfort zone than hers, Dora said, "Whatever you say." She watched as her friend waved at the twenty-something cashier behind the counter and then sashayed down the aisle toward an impressive selection of dildos.

Dora went the opposite direction, scoping out the entrance to the back room. The door behind the counter that was marked *Employees Only* was propped open, and light spilled out into the store. Once she heard Evie charming the clerk into helping her pick out the best vibrator in the store, Dora could just slip—

"Dora? Is that you?"

She froze, knowing that voice anywhere. *This is not happening. This is not happening. This is not—*

"Nice shoes. Very sexy," Luke Landucci said in a low rumble of a voice.

A ripple of pleasure rolled through her at the compliment, and she turned around. Her face had heated to almost unbearable levels, and she could barely look him in the eye when she blurted, "Bachelorette party."

"What?" he asked, his lips curved in amusement.

Dora took a moment to take in his sapphire blue eyes, sandy blond hair that was just a little too long and hanging in his eyes, and his long and lean frame with broad shoulders. She was willing to bet he was all muscle under the T-shirt he wore. Hadn't Lindy from work once told her she saw him at the gym working out every Tuesday and Thursday?

"Dora?" Luke prompted, pulling her out of her infatuation haze.

"Sorry." She shook her head as if clearing cobwebs. "We're here to find something for a bachelorette party. Our friend is getting married for the third time, and we figured we'd better up our game if we're going to top the last party we threw for her." Dora knew she was rambling. Luke Landucci, head chef of Sandbar, Pensacola's hottest new seafood restaurant, just did *something* to her. Every time she'd ever spoken to him, her insides melted and her lady parts tingled. This night was no different.

Luke's lips spread into a grin. "Imagine that. I'm here to pick up something for a bachelor party. What do you think? Edibles? Everything else seems... way too personal."

"Those boobie pops might work," Dora said, staring at the penis pops, edible undies, and flavored lubes while trying to fight the blush that was already heating her cheeks.

He chuckled. "Yeah. It's an obvious choice, but it might work."

"Dora! Did you see this?" Evie said, appearing from another aisle holding a large sparkling purple penis. "Look. It's the new version of the pink Rabbit you got last year. Remember?" Sunshine let out a little bark of agreement. Evie smiled and continued, "I talked you into buying it after—"

"We were invited to a different bachelorette party," Dora quickly finished for her. Evie had actually talked Dora into buying that Rabbit after a particularly long dry spell, followed by a horrible blind date where the guy had called his mother no less than seven times during dinner to get advice on everything from what kind of wine to order to how long he should wait to ask Dora out again. Needless to say, Dora told him they weren't a match and promptly took Evie's advice on the battery-operated purchase.

"Riiiight," Evie said, nodding. "Bachelorette party. The bride kept goosing everyone with it. I remember because Trace had been out of town and it was the most action I'd had in weeks." She winked at Luke and then glanced back and forth between the two of them. "Hey, Dora? Why haven't you and Luke ever gotten together? I bet he's a lot more fun than any Rabbit."

"Evie!" Dora hissed, ready for the floor to open up and swallow her whole. Her face burned, and she was certain she'd turned beet-red.

"That's a really good question," Luke said, his eyes sparkling with interest. "What do you say, Dora? Shall we move past appetizers?" He was referring to the way she'd sit at the bar in his restaurant before the dinner rush and he'd bring her samples of new recipes to try. She'd thought they'd been flirting, but she wasn't sure if it was only her.

He asked, "Are you busy tomorrow night?"

"I—um," Dora stammered, completely taken off guard. What if he was just teasing because of what Evie had said?

"We could go to Crabs and take a walk on the beach afterward."

Seriously? Why was Luke finally asking her out now when she couldn't go? Of course, she couldn't explain why, so she said, "I'm sorry. Evie and I have a thing." Regret pulsed through her veins. If she wasn't desperate to clear her name, she'd have jumped at the chance. Heck, she'd probably have jumped right into his arms considering her level of chill was nonexistent. "Raincheck?"

He blinked, and the mischief vanished from his gorgeous gaze. Was that disappointment that just flashed in his eyes? He blinked again and gave her an easy smile. "Sure. Next time. I'll call you."

"Okay," Dora said, her heart sinking as she watched him walk over to the counter and purchase a handful of boobie pops. As he left the store with his shopping bag in hand, Dora let out a sigh.

"I can't believe you turned him down," Evie said incredulously. "Are you crazy? We don't have a thing tomorrow. Why didn't you take him up on dinner?"

"I can't," Dora said in a hushed whisper. "I'm supposed to be laying low, remember? Weren't you just the one who said I might have someone following me? Bringing Luke into this mess is just wrong. Once we clear my name, then we'll see."

"*We'll see*," Evie mimicked and frowned at her friend. "You've got a good reason for turning him down this time, but you and I both know that you'll never go out with him unless he tracks you down and asks you again. I saw the way he looked when you shot him down. Want to bet how likely it is he'll try again?"

"He said he'd call me," Dora said, staring at the sparkly purple rabbit, but even she knew he wouldn't.

"Uh-huh. Sure, Dora. Once a man tastes a tiny bit of rejection, they retreat. You're going to have to make the first move if you want a little cookin' in your kitchen."

Dora swallowed. "I know you're probably right, but I can't do that. If he really wants a date with me, he'll ask again." She said the words, but she didn't believe them. It wasn't as if Dora was asked out every day. She wasn't Evie for goodness sake.

"And you say I'm the one who's scared?" Evie tsked, balling her hands into fists and holding them at her waist. "At least I'm not too scared to have a relationship. You know, one of these days you're going to have to finally get over your college boyfriend. That ass. He never deserved you."

"Stop. I know this is coming from a place of love, but you do know that I'm perfectly fine on my own, right?" Dora asked.

"Sure. As long as you have Mr. Sparkly here," Evie said, waving the purple dildo.

Dora held her hands up, frustrated because she would have said yes to Luke, and now her chance with him was gone. "Stop!

I can't deal with this right now. Can we please remember why we came here?"

Evie glanced around and then shrugged. "Sure. We were getting to that." She cut her gaze to the clerk and chuckled. "Lucky for us the cutie behind the counter is totally into me after our vibrator conversation," she said under her breath. "Let me go find out what he thinks of Mr. Sparkly here. I'll get him over to the display of these bad boys. You check and see if Billy's hiding out."

"I'm on it," Dora said as Sunshine lifted her head, watching as Evie sauntered over to the counter. True to her word, within moments she'd lured the cashier over to the massive display of fake penises and batted her eyelashes at him while she asked about size, speed, and customer satisfaction.

Dora chuckled to herself and tried to appear invisible as she snuck into the back room. It was just a cluttered office with an attached bathroom that smelled so bad it made her eyes water.

"Oh no, Sunshine," she said to the little dog. "I'm afraid of what we might find in there."

Sunshine let out a small whimper and tucked her nose into Dora's chest.

"You said it, sister," Dora said. She took a few steps back from the bathroom, sucked in a deep breath, and then strode forward, pushing the door all the way open.

The bathroom was empty. The only thing that remained was a broken toilet that appeared to be clogged with human waste. "Oh, gah! Gross."

Sunshine whined.

"I know. We're going," Dora whispered to the dog. After checking a small storage closet that was filled to the gills, Dora slipped back out into the store, careful to step silently until she made it to the corner next to the register as if she'd always been there.

"You know," she heard Evie say. "I think I'm going to sleep on it for a night or two. Then I'll be back."

"It's going to be the Mr. Sparkly," the clerk said with a fair amount of confidence. "It always is."

Evie giggled and flipped her hair. "Do you have personal experience with this bad boy?"

The clerk's pale face turned bright red and he started to stammer.

Dora felt a pang of sympathy for the young man, having been in a similar sticky situation moments ago. "Evie, we better get going. We're going to be late."

"Right." She gave the clerk one last flirty smile, and then met Dora near the front door and leaned in, whispering, "No luck?"

Dora shook her head. "No luck."

12

The cool sea breeze chilled Dora's skin once they made it back outside. And she was the one wearing a sweatshirt. Poor Evie wrapped her arms around herself and started to powerwalk toward her little bug. She was moving so fast, Dora, who was the taller of the two, was having trouble keeping up.

"Jeez, slow down, would ya?" Dora said, trotting to catch up with her and doing her best to not jostle Sunshine. "I'm carrying precious cargo."

Evie glanced over at her pup and her eyes softened. "She's such a good girl. Can you believe how sweet she is when we're out?"

"She a natural at the car rides, that's for sure," Dora said, walking around to the passenger side of the car. "But I think her adventure is over for the night. None of the other businesses are open right now."

"All right. Let's get home and—"

"Hold it right there," an angry voice called from the shadows.

Dora froze, squinting into the darkness, trying to make out

who was there while Sunshine's entire body vibrated as she let out a low growl.

"Get in the car, Dora," Evie demanded, already reaching for her door handle.

A gunshot fired, and Dora's heart nearly stopped as she heard the bullet whiz by, thankfully missing both of them. "Let's get out of here!" she yelled as she tried to pull her door open.

"I said to stop right there." Footsteps echoed on the pavement as the man approached them.

"We don't want any trouble," Evie said, holding her arms up in the air. "But we don't have any money. We're broke. There's nothing to take." She glanced at her little car and winced.

"The only thing I want is the flash drive," Brian said, finally stepping into the light shining down from the lamppost.

"What?" Dora asked, eyes widening as she held up her hands, trying to make it seem as if she was shocked, which wasn't hard because she never expected him to hold her at gunpoint. "Brian? Why do you have a gun on us? I—I told you, the guys who robbed Billy got it."

Brian narrowed his eyes at her and sneered. "Cut the act, Dora. I know you're not stupid. Don't insult me by assuming I am."

"I—I'm not—"

"Yes, you are. Now just tell me where the damn flash drive is."

Slowly, Dora shook her head and tried to scan the area. Was Brian alone? Where was his patrol car? And why had he fired at them? To scare them? She prayed that was all he'd intended. Though she knew that firing his gun without cause was a gross violation of the police force, and if anyone cared, he'd be in big trouble.

"I don't understand, Brian." Dora asked. "Do you think I'm in on the scheme?"

"I have my suspicions, Dora." Brian jerked his head back toward the shadowed area of the parking lot. "The patrol car is just over there. Let's say we go down to the station and get this sorted out."

Fear turned Dora's insides cold. If they got into Brian's car, would he really take them to the station? Or would she and Evie end up in some warehouse, tied up on a stone floor until they told him where to find the flash drive? Because she was pretty sure *he* was the dirty cop.

"Can't you just take her statement?" Evie asked, her voice strangely calm.

"We'll all be more comfortable and"—he scanned his gaze over her barely dressed body—"and a little warmer I suspect. That's a little scandalous even for you, isn't it, Evie?"

"It's my new look," she said defiantly. If there was one thing Evie hated, it was when men tried to tell her how to dress or shamed her for her short skirts. "Got a problem with that, *Officer Brian*?"

"Nope. But I bet Trace won't appreciate his girl walking around like a two-bit hooker," he said with a chuckle.

"Why you—" Evie lunged for him, her arms outstretched as if she was going to tackle him or scratch his eyes out.

"Evie! No!" Dora called, her heart in her throat as she watched her bestie try to assault an officer of the law.

"Arf!" Sunshine jumped out of Dora's hands and ran toward Evie, but just before she reached her mistress's side, she turned and also lunged for Brian, her teeth bared. Unlike Evie, Sunshine actually made contact, and Brian let out a yelp and kicked out, catching the dog's back end with his boot. Sunshine went flying about ten feet.

Evie spun just before she got to Brian and changed course, reaching down to pick up her small dog, who was now panting and glaring at Brian.

"That's it," Brian said, recklessly waving his firearm in Evie and then Dora's direction. "Both of you, in the car. Right now, or I'm calling back up. If that happens, then your chance to tell your story will be delayed, and you both will be processed through the system." He glared at Sunshine. "And that one will end up at animal control. If you're lucky, they won't adopt her out before you're released."

"Why, you no good, dirty, piece of monkey spit!" Evie said, clutching Sunshine. "What is wrong with you, you sick bastard?"

He sneered at her and then held out his leg. "Looks like your little beast drew blood. I believe they kill dogs who bite around these parts."

Dora stared down at his pasty white ankle and rolled her eyes when she saw the tiniest trickle of blood. "You probably scraped your leg on Sunshine's collar when you kicked her."

"Shut up and get in the car." He circled around, still holding his gun, so that Dora and Evie had no choice but to walk toward the cruiser that was still sitting in the shadows.

13

The back of Brian's patrol car had an odor of urine so strong even Sunshine crinkled her nose. Dora gave the pup a sympathetic look.

"Jeez, Brian," Evie said. "Get an air freshener already. Maybe one of those candle ones, like ocean calm. Or if fruity is your thing, they have a Tahiti sunset that has the relaxing aroma of coconut. Might chill out the perps, you know what I'm saying? There's always new car smell, too." She chuckled as Brian pulled out onto the highway.

Dora's stomach sank when she realized they were headed in the opposite direction of the police station.

Evie continued her riff, "But that's such a crock, right? Who even knows what that smells like? Because no fool buys a brand-new car these days. Although..." Evie took a moment to glance around at the torn leather of the back seat and frowned as her gaze fixated on a dark stain on the carpet that Dora really hoped wasn't blood. "Have you seen the state of this back seat lately? It might be time for you to trade this puppy, no offense Sunshine, in. Or at least get it de—"

"Shut! Up!" Brian finally yelled.

Dora and Evie exchanged wide-eyed glances, and Dora knew her friend was rambling this time because she was nervous. She reached over and grabbed Evie's hand to squeeze it tight, and Sunshine let out a small whine as she laid her head on her paws in Evie's lap.

Dora asked, "Where are you taking us?"

"Hmpf," Brian's eyes appeared darker than Dora remembered as he glared at her in the rearview mirror. "You see far too much for your own good."

Dora was afraid that wasn't entirely true, because if she'd had sharper eyes, she would have noticed the money laundering scheme of Marco's a lot sooner and figured out Brian was a crook instead of the nice guy next door.

Evie let out a huff of exasperation. "You really have to stop underestimating people." She winked at Dora. "Even *I* know you're not taking us the right way for the police station."

Dora never liked the way Evie downplayed her intelligence, especially when she was feeling depressed about her latest loss of employment, but she had to admit Evie did know how to use the fact that most people thought she was a ditzy blonde to her advantage. And it might come in handy. She nudged Evie with her elbow and mouthed, *Way to go.*

She eyed Sunshine, who was fast becoming a solid member of their team. Dora still wasn't sure how the tiny dog knew how to sort mail, but she was positive everyone would underestimate the little ball of fur too.

Her mind raced as she tried to figure out the best way to get them free. While she didn't think Brian would kill them, she also hadn't believed he'd hold her at gunpoint either. No, it was best if she prepared for the worst. Glancing down at her shoes, she recalled how earlier she'd joked she could use one of the stilettos she was wearing as a weapon, and at the moment, it didn't seem like a bad idea.

She reached down, pulled a shoe from her foot, and gripped it tightly in her hand as Brian slowed the car. Evie was wearing heels too, although they were platforms, but she took Dora's lead and removed a shoe as well.

Brian pulled into the strip mall where Evie used to work and drove around back to the service entrances. He parked the car close to a door that read, *Price Dry Cleaners,* where Evie had worked until two days earlier.

Evie's jaw dropped. "Fred is on the take?"

Brian turned to look over his seat at Dora and chuckled. He tapped his temple as if they were still buddies. "Rocket scientist, that one."

Sunshine growled at Brian as Dora gripped her shoe tighter, and she felt her anger flood her veins along with the adrenaline she was going to need to help her overpower the jerk who had just insulted her best friend.

Brian was still laughing to himself as he got out of the car and greeted a man who'd emerged from the dry cleaners. The guy was wearing a T-shirt that was so tight it was on the verge of ripping if he flexed, and the solid mass of muscle it revealed, as well as the gun strapped to his side, made things very clear. Two high heels were not going to be effective weapons.

"Damn it," Dora muttered. "Put your shoe back on."

Evie let out a sigh. "I was so looking forward to a little blunt trauma. Might have improved Brian's attitude toward women."

Sunshine let out a yap of agreement as the hulking man pulled Evie's door open and leaned in to take a look at them.

"Jock?" Evie asked. The man's smile became a lecherous grin as he made no attempt at hiding the fact he was scanning Evie's assets in her red dress. "Unbelievable," Evie scoffed. "And to think I bought your misunderstood-for-your-appearance act. You are the thug everyone thinks you are."

He grabbed Evie's hand to help her out of the car and bit his lower lip once she was standing and he could get a good look at her. "And your story doesn't pan out either. You're every bit the sexpot I expected."

"Ugh, I definitely should have swiped no-way-in-hell on your dating profile when I had the chance."

During Evie and Jock's exchange, Dora managed to get herself out of the car to stand next to her friend. Brian pulled the door to the dry cleaners open and waved his gun at the women before he said in a tone dripping with sarcasm, "*Ladies*, after you."

Dora and Evie were led to an office, and Brian instructed them to sit in the two chairs. Dora went to sit behind the desk where there was a chair with roller wheels, but Brian waved to a plain stationary chair with no arms and barked out, "Over here."

Evie took the rolling chair, and Sunshine jumped out of Dora's arms to sit in Evie's lap, making her think the little dog knew which seat would be better equipped for breaking them free.

"Now," Brian growled out. "If Dora here can tell me where to find the flash drive, this can be a painless experience."

Dora jumped when she heard the rip of duct tape being pulled from a roll and saw Jock bite off a long strip. She said, "If I had it, I'd give it to you, I swear." She needed to buy time and added, "You got Billy's mail bag. If it wasn't in there, then maybe it will be in Monday's mail."

Brian glared at her, but Dora could see he was considering what she'd said, which was good because the way things were headed, she thought she just bought Evie and herself two more days of life. But as she looked over at Evie and took in her skimpy red dress, she remembered what they'd been doing out of hiding in the first place, and it occurred to her that Billy might not have the same amount of time.

14

"**Y**ou'd better hope that flash drive is in Monday's mail," Brian said to Dora. He leaned in so close that she could smell the garlic on his breath, and it made her stomach turn. "Because I got a good look at the security tapes from Two to Mango, and it seems like you killed Steve Franklin."

"But she didn't!" Evie cried.

Brian stepped back from Dora and grinned at her before he looked at Evie and shrugged. "Along with a cop's expert testimony, no jury would have a reason to believe otherwise." He sneered at Dora. "You've got yourself in a pickle, young lady. But you can make this nightmare for you and your friend go away. All I need is the flash drive."

Real tears burned in Dora's eyes, because she was going to jail either way. Without that flash drive as evidence, she had no doubt Marco would pin her for the money laundering scheme instead of Steve's death. She whimpered and then repeated, "If I had it, I'd give it to you. I swear!"

It was not the answer Brian was looking for, and he barked out to Jock, "Restrain them."

Jock approached Evie first, and Sunshine growled. Brian said, "Do the mutt, too."

Evie gasped and clutched the dog tighter. "You can't use duct tape on Sunshine! It'll rip her fur out."

"She's right," Dora said. "You can't possibly be that cruel. There must be another way." She glanced around the room, panicked for the little dog, and spotted a necktie laying on a filing cabinet. "How about that tie? You can loop it through Sunshine's collar and then tie her to the leg of the desk. She won't be able to go anywhere then."

Jock said, "She's right boss." He tilted his head at Sunshine, who did the same to him, and in that universal dog voice nobody would ever expect from a guy like Jock, he said, "I won't hurt you, little cutie wooty."

Dora managed to cover her snort of laughter with a cough, while Evie eyed Jock with skepticism.

Brian rolled his eyes to the ceiling. "Just restrain them."

Five minutes later, Dora and Evie were taped to their chairs and Sunshine was on a short leash.

When the men left them, Dora yanked on her arms and legs with the hope the tape would give, but after struggling for a few moments all it proved to her was that she wasn't getting free. "Evie, can Sunshine bite the tape on your arms or ankles?"

The dog strained against her collar, but she'd been tied to a front leg of the desk and couldn't quite reach Evie. Dora's hope was deflated, and she let her tears fall in hot streams down her cheeks. She'd been so determined to save Evie and herself she hadn't let frustration take over. But now... "Evie, I'm so sorry." A sob escaped before she got control again. "You've been the best friend ever. Nobody else would have stuck through this with me, and I"—she hiccupped—"I can't believe we're going to end like this."

"You don't think they're going to kill us, do you?"

Dora sniffed, "Not yet, but how are we going to get out of this one?"

"I don't know, but I do know that giving up is not the answer," Evie said with authority. "Don't you wimp out on me now, Dora Winslow."

Dora didn't want to. She was used to being the strong one, although, Evie was just as strong in her own way. While she usually let Dora be the bossy one, she had proven she could take the lead when necessary.

Evie gasped. "We may not be able to escape, but I know how we're going to get some information. Sunshine, it's time for doggy and me yoga."

"What?" Dora shook her head. "Look, I know you think communing with your inner chi or whatever might provide insight, but you aren't seriously going to make your dog practice yoga right now, are you?"

"Yes," Evie said with authority. "And let me tell you why. Fred loved to spy on me. See that TV screen on the wall?"

Dora glanced over her shoulder at the screen that was across from the desk where Evie was seated. "It's not on."

"No, but the remote for it is on the desk." Evie winked at Sunshine. "Are you limbered up?"

Sunshine let out a little growl as a *yes*.

The controls were on the desk. Neither of them could reach it, and Sunshine couldn't jump up on it because she was tied to the table leg. Dora shook her head, unable to fathom how Evie expected to get to the remote. "But—"

"Mountain pose," Evie commanded. The dog lifted her front legs up to extend like a standing human. "Very good, Sunshine. Someone's been practicing. Dora, can you see this?"

"Evie, please." Dora pleaded.

"Right. Sorry." She returned her gaze to the dog, who wasn't tall enough to see the top of the desk. "Reach for the sky and hit that remote."

The dog lifted her front paws up over her little head and dropped them down onto the desk. One hit the remote, and Dora noticed the word *audio* pop up on the screen before the dog landed back on all fours and the controls went skittering across the room.

"Darn it," Evie said.

But Dora heard something else clatter and shook her head. "Shhh."

Brian's voice came through the television speaker. "—Miss Morris. This is getting ridiculous."

Jock said, "You know I don't do animal cruelty. It's in the contract."

Brian let out a noise of disgust. "That's something. A goon with morals."

"You got a problem with that?" Jock challenged.

Brian sighed. "No, you jackass. But you get to keep the dog. I already have enough to deal with."

Evie's wide eyes told Dora they were thinking the same thing. Jock may be keeping the dog because Dora and Evie would no longer be able to. And she didn't think it was because they were going to be out of town.

For a moment, Dora wondered who Miss Morris was, but she didn't have time to ponder it because Brian said, "I'll stake out Evie's house for Monday's mail. We'll keep them alive until I get the flash drive... just in case."

"Whattaya want me to do with the mailman?"

"Billy?" Brian chuckled. "The gator will run out of food Sunday night, and come Monday there won't be a scrap of him left."

Evie's lower lip trembled as she and Dora stared at each

other in fear for Billy, the kind mail carrier. And it occurred to Dora that she now knew where the mailman was. An alligator park was one of the businesses that had been in Marco's files of cooked books. But a fat lot of good it did them if they couldn't escape in time to save him. Or themselves.

15

A t some point in the night, Dora and Evie dozed off, and Evie woke to the sound of someone rustling around in the main lobby of the dry cleaners. She determined Brian and Jock were gone when she heard the new girl, who must have taken her place, talking to herself as she ran through the opening checklist.

"Lights on," the girl said. Evie looked over and noticed Dora was awake too. She heard the girl also say, "Unlock the clerk safe for my cash drawer." Fred had a small safe for the clerks to keep the register drawer. The deposit at the end of the day went into a slot in a bigger safe that only Fred had access to.

The girl continued, "One to the right, two to the left and... Wait. What's the next number? Darn it. One, two...?" There was silence for a moment, and it made Dora want to shout 'three' to her. But then the girl giggled. "Brain fart. Where was I?" She blew out a long breath, apparently trying again. "One to the right, two to the left, and three to the right. Yes!" They heard rattling that was likely change in the plastic drawer, and then the girl said, "Unlock the door. Huh? What's this? I guess I'm supposed to read Fred's note. Hmpf. That's not on my opening check list." She let out a big sigh as if reading a note was a burden. Which Evie assumed might be for her. "*Dear New Girl.* Really? Fred doesn't even know my name?" She huffed. "*Personality disorder therapy has begun in the office next door. Ignore anything you hear.*"

Dora gasped. "She's not going to believe that bull, is she?"

Evie raised her eyebrows. "Her safe combination is one, two, three, and she couldn't remember it."

"Good point," Dora conceded. "There goes the calling-for-help idea."

Evie watched as Dora's eyes filled with tears, and her heart ached for her friend, who seemed to be giving up hope.

Dora's voice was shaky as she asked, "What is your biggest regret in life?"

"What?" It was worse than Evie had feared. Dora *had* given up and was sure they were going to die. "No, Dora –"

"Not having children," Dora interrupted. "I think I would have been a great mother."

Evie took stock of her best friend. Tears were running down her face with streaks of mascara marking the trail. She'd been strong and capable until they'd been restrained last night, but now she was falling apart. Evie knew her friend had cried herself to sleep too. And who could blame her? In the span of three days, Dora had discovered a money laundering scheme, accidently killed her boss, gotten a mailman kidnapped, done a lap dance that would make a real stripper blush, and was now duct taped to a chair. But even so, it was heartbreaking for Evie to see her best friend give up hope.

Evie said, "You *will* be a great mother one day. I can just see little number-crunching chefs telling my free-spirited musician kids what to do at playgroup."

The bell to the front door jingled, and Evie stopped talking to listen. The new clerk might believe the ridiculous therapy excuse, but maybe a rational customer wouldn't.

"Thank god you're open," said a familiar voice.

Dora gasped. "Is that—"

"*Luke,*" Evie said as she recognized the voice and listened.

"Hey!" The clerk yelled. "You can't—"

"My chef's jacket is back here somewhere!"

"Here!" Dora cried out, hoping her volume was loud enough to lead him to the office.

The door burst open, and he rushed in and slammed it behind him. He yelled, "Found it! Be out in a minute."

"Oh. Okay," the girl said in a chipper voice as if all was well. "Hey, do you think you could watch the front for me while I run to Starbucks?" Her voice turned dramatic. "I'm just *dyyying* for a coffee." Before Luke could answer, she said, "Be right back!"

Luke rushed over to Dora and grabbed her face. "Are you hurt?"

Fresh tears were in Dora's eyes, and Evie suspected they were from relief as her friend shook her head.

"I'm going to get you out of here. Hold on." Luke moved over to the desk and yanked open drawers, items clattering as he searched for something to use to release them.

Evie asked, "How did you know we were here?"

"I heard the gunshot last night as I was leaving the adult toy shop, and when I noticed the man talking to you, I hid behind a dumpster and watched the whole thing." Luke grabbed a pair of scissors and went to work cutting at Dora's restraints. "I've been outside waiting for my chance to come get you. Whatever trouble you're in, Dora..." He paused, and it was a movie moment. At least it felt that way when his voice turned steely as he added, "I'll get you out of it."

Dora's hands were finally free, and she placed one on Luke's cheek. "You're going to save me?"

While the moment was certainly touching and definitely the kind of thing Evie was happy for her friend to experience, she'd been stuck to her chair for far too long to be patient, and she asked, "Any chance you could save me too?"

Luke finished cutting Dora free and moved to Evie. She couldn't help noticing how well he filled out the black T-shirt that hugged his muscular chest in all the right ways as he said, "My car is out back. I'm going to take you to my place where we can regroup and figure out a plan."

Evie's stomach grumbled. Knowing she was going to squeeze into the tight red dress to go to the strip club the night before, she hadn't eaten much dinner, and poor Sunshine was probably starving for breakfast. "Can we hit that Starbucks drive thru on the way?"

Luke chuckled. "Do you think I'm going to allow that? I'll make you the best darn cappuccino this side of the ocean once we get to my place."

"And scones?" Dora asked. "Please tell me you'll make those cranberry orange scones I tasted last week because they were soooo good."

Evie twirled her hands to make sure her wrists still worked as she watched Dora's transformation from accepting her impending death to flirting with chef Luke. It was one she was happy to see. Once Luke untied Sunshine, Evie scooped her up, and they followed Dora and her knight out the back door.

16

D ora wrapped the white button-down shirt of Luke's a little tighter around her body and tucked a leg under her bottom as she perched on a bar stool at Luke's kitchen island. The best cappuccino she'd ever had warmed her hands as she held the cup. She'd taken a long hot shower at his place and even washed her hair using his shampoo, which meant she now had a lingering woodsy scent she associated with him surrounding her. It was comforting and something she never expected could make her feel so good. Letting a man take care of her wasn't a luxury Dora was used to.

Bacon sizzled in a pan, and the scent of cranberry orange scones wafted from the oven as Luke made breakfast for them. Sunshine was chomping on a bowl full of dry dog food Luke had gotten from a neighbor, and Evie was taking her turn in the shower. It gave Dora time to explain the mess she'd gotten them into.

"It all started with a job that was too good to be true." She gazed into Luke's sapphire-blue eyes as she told him how she'd discovered the money laundering scheme and snuck the flash drive of files into Evie's package just before the accidental shooting that had sent her running in fear.

She explained how Billy had been intercepted and kidnapped, and that the flash drive was actually in a package on its way to New Orleans. She told him about Brian's deception. And then she told him a condensed version of searching for Billy at the strip club before running into him at the sex shop. She had just finished her story when Evie emerged from the bathroom in a blue shirt like the one Dora was wearing.

Luke set two plates down for the women and remained standing on his side of the island to face them. "So, you need to get to New Orleans undetected to get the flash drive," he said. "Once you have it, you can take it to someone you trust and prove your innocence and uncover the whole scheme."

"That sounds about right, but there's one more thing," Dora said. "We've got to save Billy first."

"And we know where he is," Evie added. She bit into a piece of bacon and let out a moan of satisfaction.

"He's at an alligator park the Franklins—well, Marco Franklin—owns, and he's safe until the gators run out of food tonight," Dora said.

Luke pulled a phone out of his back pocket, and Dora had a moment of panic, not sure she could trust him. He was a man she'd just confessed to after all. "Wait!"

He frowned in question for a second and then seemed to understand. He gave her a reassuring smile. "I'm just calling my assistant to let her know I'm not coming in to work tonight. I think you ladies need my help."

Dora relaxed, and warmth filled her heart at his kindness. But then a chill took over. "I can't let you do that. It would put you in danger too."

"I believe rescuing you from the dry cleaners already has." Luke winked at her and hit Call on his phone.

He was right, and it made Dora's stomach knot up. She couldn't believe she'd managed to involve another person she cared about in her situation. While Dora picked at her eggs, Evie chowed down. She wasn't quite sure Evie had a grasp on the fact they'd barely escaped losing their lives, but she wasn't about to ruin her friend's appetite. At least someone could make use of the energy Luke's breakfast provided.

Luke ended his call and leaned across the counter to tip Dora's chin up so he could gaze into her eyes. "You need to eat."

"I know." She let out a breath as tears threatened to come. "I'm just—"

"Scared," Luke said.

She nodded, and he grabbed her hand to squeeze her fingers.

He said, "It's okay to be scared, but food will help keep you alert. Today we're going to rescue Billy, and I'm going to send you on your way to New Orleans safe and sound. Got it?"

Dora nodded again, and this time she almost meant it. She scooped up a forkful of eggs and put them in her mouth in an attempt to get some protein in her body. She believed Luke could and would do what he said. It was a sobering thought, though, because it meant she might not see him again for a long time.

"Can I have more bacon?" Evie asked over a mouthful of food as if Dora and Luke were discussing a shopping list. "And don't you think those scones might be done, Romeo?"

Luke shook his head and rescued the scones before shoveling more eggs and bacon onto Evie's plate. He reached over and grabbed a scone with a pair of tongs and placed it on Dora's plate. The butter dish scraped across the counter, and he pushed it at her with a smile. Then he said, "Can you believe I finally get the nerve to ask Dora out and she's going to skip town on me?"

"I know, right?" Evie replied, trying to help him lighten the mood. But then she looked at Dora and got serious. "It's not going to be forever. You and I have two great men who live here. We're coming back to clear your name as soon as we can."

Dora smiled, because while she and Luke hadn't even kissed, the way he'd rescued them and put himself in danger for her told her she had found a great man. She was just as determined to return to Luke as Evie was to come back to Trace. She smeared butter on her scone and bit into the steamy goodness. The flavor did more than warm her insides. It warmed her heart. Maybe it was the power of food, or maybe, she dared to hope, it was the power of love, because she had new confidence everything was going to turn out okay.

～

"Ugh," exclaimed Dora as she pinched her nose. Florida heat and humidity, combined with the alligator-filled swampy waters, gave off a ripe stench that made her eyes water. She and Evie, along with Luke, were checking out the gator park where they suspected Billy was being kept. After a quick trip to Target, Dora and Evie were decked out in shorts, or a short skirt in Evie's case, T-shirts, and practical shoes like a typical tourist. They were there as visitors so they could come up with a plan for after hours when they returned to set Billy free.

Dora glanced over at Evie and checked the bag she was carrying. Sunshine was not allowed into the alligator park, so they'd hidden her in a backpack Luke had. But Dora wasn't so sure Sunshine had an awareness of how important it was to stay hidden. As if to validate her fear, Sunshine poked her nose out of the top of the bag. Dora glared at the little pup, and she ducked her head back down in fear.

"Evie, you've got to keep your dog in check," she hissed at her friend.

"She's fine." Evie's paper map rustled as she unfolded it, and she hammed it up playing her role as a tourist. "Look at this! Oh, my. So many gators. So little time." She glanced at a man walking toward them. "Can you believe this place?"

He smiled at her, which only opened the door for more of Evie's dramatics. She grabbed his arm and suddenly had a southern accent. "My friends and I are here on vacation from Tennessee," she drawled. "What's the best part of this park, would you say?"

"Well, I'm a big fan of the gator wrestling." He turned and pointed off to the left. "It's right over there."

"Oh, my," Evie said, her accent getting thicker as she rubbed his forearm. "I bet you'd be really good at that, too."

"Oh—" The man's face blushed a nice shade of Florida sunburn. "Well, I'm not sure—"

"Oh, pshaw!" Evie giggled. "I don't suppose you'd mind taking our picture, would you?"

"Uh, I—I'm not that good with cameras." He started backing away, and Dora thought Evie might have overdone it.

But Evie had no intention of letting the man get away. She cried out, "Great!" and shoved her phone into the guy's hands. "Make sure you take a bunch from all angles. We wouldn't want any unfortunate double chins or tummy rolls when we post to Insta, right?"

"Insta?" the older man asked, confusion swimming in his eyes.

"Aren't you sweet?" Evie giggled and adjusted the phone, showing him where to hit the button. "Remember now, act like a photographer on a mission. Plenty of angles, high and low."

Evie grabbed Dora, nearly knocking her off her feet as she pulled her to the fence. Dora glanced across the facility, spotting

Luke. Evie and Dora were supposed to create enough of a minor distraction so that he could get a feel for where they should be looking for Billy. So far, the plan was right on track, and Dora watched him sneak into a side door that was clearly marked *Employees Only*.

"Dora!" Evie gave her friend a knowing grin. "Hop up on the fence railing. That will make it a much better shot."

Dora eyed the enclosure and the lazy gators. None of them were particularly close, but Dora had seen enough zoo snapshots gone wrong that she shook her head. "I'm not sure that's a good idea, Evie," she whispered into her friend's ear. "I think we should be on the safe side and just stand here."

"Dora." Evie sucked in an impatient breath. "How is that going to create a distraction?" She pumped her eyebrows. "We need to live a little dangerously. Just hook your feet between the bars. You're not that clumsy. It's fine. Come on."

Dora decided she had a point. If they were doing something that appeared dangerous, people would definitely watch. Dora glanced back at the enclosure one more time, just to reassure herself that none of the gators were looking especially hungry, and then lifted herself up, careful to brace her feet on the bottom railing.

"There you go," Evie said with a bright smile, her eyes twinkling with mischief. She handed Dora the backpack that housed Sunshine. "Open up the flap so she can stick her head out."

Dora did as she was told. "Come on, Sunshine. Picture time."

The pup popped up out of the pack, her hair sticking up all over the place as she swung her head from side to side, getting a good look at her surroundings.

"Sorry about this," Dora whispered to the dog as she tried to finger comb the pup's wild hair into submission. "I told your mom we needed a proper puppy purse, the kind with vents that would give you more air."

"Stop. It's not like I zipped her in there," Evie said, climbing up to take her spot next to Dora. She patted Sunshine on the head. "You're okay, right, baby?"

The dog stuck her tongue out and licked Evie's hand.

"Okay, that's enough. We need to hold still so the nice man can take our picture," Dora said, pulling the pack and Sunshine in close to her body.

"Okay, Mr. Helpful," Evie said, poking a shoulder forward and leaning down a little to flash the older man a bit of cleavage to go with her flirty smile. "We need plenty of shots to pick from, so go ahead and snap a bunch. 'Kay?"

"What?" he asked, staring at the phone like it was some alien technology he'd never used before.

"You know, we need to smize and capture all of our best angles." Evie nudged Dora. "Remember to smize."

Dora rolled her eyes at the Tyra Banks reference. Evie had watched way too much *America's Next Top Model*, which meant Dora knew that *smize* was the term meaning to smile using your eyes as well as your mouth. She still wasn't sure how that was possible.

"Do it, Dora," she whispered under her breath. "You don't want to be the crabby one when we show these to our kids twenty years from now."

Kids, Dora thought. She'd always wanted two. A boy and a girl, two years apart, named Brandon and Callie. Both with blond hair and blue eyes just like Luke. *Gah!* She shook her head, trying to force the thoughts from her mind. What was she doing? Her stomach started to ache with the knowledge the pretty little picture she'd conjured for herself was likely never to come true. And it sure as heck wouldn't if they didn't at least try to get out of the mess she'd gotten both of them into.

"Dora, smize!" Evie elbowed her.

The backpack jostled and nearly slipped right out of Dora's hands. Sunshine let out a yelp and scrambled up onto Dora's shoulder. But she overshot and went flying right into the alligator enclosure.

"Sunshine! Oh my god!" Without even a second thought, Dora dropped the pack and followed Sunshine over the fence into the shallow water. The warm water came up to her mid-calf, soaking her tennis shoes, but Dora didn't give them one extra thought. Sunshine was standing on a small rock, soaked to the bone and completely still as if she was frozen by fear.

"My baby!" Evie called and splashed into the enclosure as well. She let out a shriek and launched herself back at the fence.

"Evie!" Dora switched direction and headed toward her friend, noting a small four-foot alligator heading for the spot right where Evie had been a few seconds before.

"No! Get Sunshine," Evie ordered with a sob as she pointed at her baby.

"Right." With her heart hammering against her breastbone, Dora tried to ignore the fact that at least one gator was nearby and hurried toward Sunshine. The pup was shaking fiercely and breathing hard. "I've got you, Sunshine," she said, reaching out for the pup.

Sunshine let out a yelp and shot forward, right into the water with a splash.

Dora felt rather than saw the movement behind her.

"Watch out!" Evie cried, her voice so high-pitched she'd gone supersonic.

There was no time to assess the situation. If she didn't grab the dog, Dora was certain she was going to witness the poor thing becoming a gator snack. That was something she'd never let happen. Adrenaline shot her forward, and she reached down, grabbed the small dog, and took off for the fence.

"No! Dora, go right, go right!" Evie screamed.

Dora didn't hesitate. She immediately turned and lengthened her stride, slogging through the water while clutching Sunshine, who'd buried her head in Dora's chest. The poor baby was still shaking, but Dora knew without a doubt, she wasn't going anywhere this time. The fence was only a few feet away when Dora heard a sloshing behind her. *Gator!*

"Toss Sunshine to me," Luke ordered after appearing out of nowhere on the other side of the fence.

Dora's entire body was straining to outrun the gator behind her, and even though she was terrified, she tossed Sunshine and launched herself at the fence. Her fingers latched onto the top rung, and before she could find purchase with her feet, two familiar hands helped yank her over the edge. Dora hit the ground face-first, but she'd never felt so relieved to eat dirt than she did in that moment.

"Dora!" Evie slid to the ground, lying on Dora's back and wrapping her arms around her friend. "Are you all right? You saved Sunshine. Thank you! Thank you!"

"Oof." Dora pushed herself and Evie up, spitting the dirt out of her mouth, and frowned at her friend. Evie must have a huge adrenaline spike of her own to be able to yank Dora from the gator pond. She said in relief, "I'm okay." But she wasn't. Not really. Her hands were shaking so hard she pressed them together just to try to still them. It didn't work. And even though it was at least ninety degrees, her skin was cold and clammy, and the world started to spin.

Luke approached and handed Sunshine to Evie. Sunshine let out a yelp, and Evie clutched her dog to her chest, tears streaming down her face.

"I'm so sorry, sweetheart," Evie said to the dog. "You must be so scared. It's okay. Mommy has you now." She pressed her lips to the dog's head, giving her a kiss, but then blew a raspberry as she wrinkled her nose. "Wow. You smell really bad, little girl. No way you're sharing my bed until you get a bath."

"Get them on their feet," a man barked out.

Cold dread ran through Dora's veins. The 'distraction' they'd staged had turned into a full-fledged nightmare that had drawn the attention of security. This was it. Both of them were going to get arrested, and after all they'd done to avoid it, Dora would still need to think about finding a bitch to protect her in prison. She shuddered.

"No! I'm too pretty for jail," Evie blurted, scrambling to her feet and backing away, still clutching Sunshine. "Besides, I can't orphan my dog. She has separation anxiety."

"Ma'am," the man in uniform said with exasperation. "We're not taking you to prison. We're—"

"It's not my fault. I was just trying to get a picture," Evie whined.

"Miss, can you get to your feet?" another man asked Dora, his tone clearly running out of patience.

"I think so." Dora's limbs were still wobbly after the adrenaline rush, but she did finally get her feet under her just in time to see one of the security guards raise his weapon. "Don't shoot!" she yelled as the contents of her stomach lurched dangerously up her throat.

The uniformed man drew his eyebrows together and frowned at her as he handed the weapon off to another officer. "No one is going to shoot you miss. The gun is for the alligators."

"You're going to shoot them?" Dora asked while still holding her hands in the air. "No. You can't!" she cried, fearing for the innocent reptiles who hadn't done anything but be who they were. "We're safe now. No need to make matters worse. No one is going back in the enclosure. I can promise you that." Or at least Dora wasn't. Evie's gaze was darting around, clearly looking for an escape route.

"Why would we shoot them?" The officer seemed genuinely confused. "That's only done in extreme cases. If Harry hadn't gotten in there and distracted those guys, it might've been necessary, but luckily, my boy over there"—he held up his hands and managed to do air quotes while holding a gun—"is *one* with the gators."

Dora blinked at him. "What?"

His mouth tightened, and he grabbed her by the upper arm, marching her over to the fence. "See those two gators just lying there, unmoving?"

Dora felt a lump form in her throat as she nodded.

"Harry and Pauly got 'em. There's tape wrapped around their snouts now until we inspect the enclosure and make sure neither of them will be a danger after their exciting day." He scowled at her. "You didn't feed them anything, did you?"

"What? No!" Dora glanced over at Evie and Sunshine. Evie looked like she'd swallowed a canary. What the heck was she up to? Dora narrowed her eyes at her friend. What kind of trouble was coming next? She turned to the man. "I apologize. This was obviously a huge mistake. We just... ah... my friend's dog has separation anxiety," she said lamely.

"You and your friend will be escorted out now." He waved a couple of other security officers over. "Make sure these two make it outside the grounds and put a ban on them at the front gate. They've caused enough trouble."

"We really are sorry," Dora mumbled as the security guard grabbed her wrist and started leading her toward the park entrance. She noticed another one had grabbed Evie, but Luke was nowhere to be found. Had they messed up so badly that he'd bailed? If he had, she could hardly blame him. Why would he spend his time helping her out? It wasn't as if they were dating or anything.

A small voice in the back of her head whispered, *He's doing it to help Billy. Not you.*

That sounded about right. Luke was a good guy. He wouldn't let anyone kill Billy. Maybe he hadn't disappeared without a trace. Maybe he was using this highly effective distraction to get intel on the park. She closed her eyes and sucked in a deep breath, praying that was the truth.

The security guards shoved both Evie and Dora out through the exit of the park. The tall one that had been manhandling Dora said, "Please don't come back. Ever. This isn't a playground. You, your friend, and your dog were lucky today. This could've gone down much worse."

Evie placed a soft hand on his forearm. "We are so sorry, sir. We didn't mean to slip into the enclosure. Overzealous touristing, I suppose." She batted her eyelashes at him. "Thank you for keeping my friend and my puppy safe. You and your coworkers are *heroes*."

Dora rolled her eyes as she watched the guard give Evie a smile. His eyes raked over her before he said, "Anytime, gorgeous. Just try to stay out of trouble in the future, okay? This world would be a dimmer place without all your sparkle."

Evie giggled, while Dora resisted the urge to gag. Her friend placed her palm on the guard's chest, playing her act for all she was worth. "You're a sweetie, officer...?"

"Matt. You can call me Matt." He shrugged his shoulders, "And I'm not really a cop." He practically glowed with pleasure as he smiled down at her.

"You might as well be. *Officer* Matt," she cooed. "Would you do me a favor?"

"Sure, anything," he said with a hitch in his voice as he leaned in expectantly.

Evie glanced away shyly, and when she looked back at him, she'd caught her lower lip between her teeth. "I... ah, well, I was supposed to be home sick today, and if my boss gets wind I was

out at a gator park, there's no telling what she'll do. I was
wondering if you could make sure this stays under wraps. No
press and no report to the police? She has ways of finding out
these things, and... Well, if they find out I was here, I'll be
unemployed, all because I needed a mental health day." She let
out a dramatic sigh.

Are those tears in Evie's eyes? Dora wondered. Maybe those
acting classes had paid off.

Dora had to give it to her. The woman was finding a way to
keep their antics on the down-low so that Brian and any other
corrupt cops at the station wouldn't hear about it. Dora would
have to do something nice for her later, like bake her cupcakes
or something. If only they had the time for that.

"You got it, cutie," Matt said in that overconfident voice men
tended to get when they were sure they were well on their way
to scoring some action. "How about you give me your number,
and I'll make sure all of this gets swept under the rug."

Dora gritted her teeth and didn't miss the flash of annoyance
in Evie's gaze. But it was there one moment and gone the next.
Dora was certain Matt didn't notice. He was too busy staring at
Evie's chest anyway.

"Sure, doll," Evie purred in a fake voice. Then she rattled off
a phone number Dora didn't recognize. "Can't wait for that
date." Evie winked and jerked her head at Dora. "Let's get out of
here before *Officer* Matt gets chastised for flirting with the
troublemakers."

"You don't have to ask me twice," Dora said, striding past
Matt and slipping her arm through Evie's. "I desperately need a
shower. Let's go."

Matt whistled to himself as he made his way back into the
alligator park, while Evie and Dora made their way across the
parking lot, an uneasy silence settling between them. Dora had
no idea what to say to her friend. What if something had

happened to Sunshine while she'd been the one holding the little dog? The thought was too horrific to even entertain. She wrapped her arms around herself and slumped against Luke's car while they waited for him to show up.

Dora closed her eyes and tilted her face toward the sun, hoping the bright rays would warm the chill that had taken over her body. Despite the hot afternoon, after the incident in the gator enclosure, Dora's insides had turned to ice.

Dora could hear Evie murmuring to Sunshine that everything was okay now. A moment later, Dora heard footsteps, right before she felt a pair of thin arms come around her and hold on tight.

"Oh my god, Dora," Evie said. "I was so scared for both of you. Thank god you're both okay."

Dora let out a small sob and hugged her friend just as tightly. "No. I'm the one who's sorry, Evie. I don't know how I lost control of Sunshine. If anything had happened to her—" Dora's throat closed, and she was unable to finish her apology.

"No. I'm sorry. I should've listened to you and gotten a better dog carrier." A full body shudder ran through her as she pulled away. "I can't stop picturing her in the jaws of one of those beasts."

Dora pulled back and squeezed Evie's hands. "She's okay. I'm okay. And you were brilliant with *Officer* Matt. Try not to stress too hard about this, okay? We can hit the drive-thru ice cream place and get triple scoops of chocolate caramel with zero guilt. As soon as we figure out where Luke is." She really hoped he hadn't skipped out on them, although she wouldn't blame him. She had a sinking feeling he had because she was used to men letting her down. Dora pulled slightly back from Evie and said, "Okay?"

Evie nodded and wiped at her damp eyes. "That sounds good. With hot fudge and extra whipped cream."

Dora chuckled. "Obviously."

"What's this I hear about ice cream?" Luke's voice sounded from behind them, and Dora's heart soared.

"We need a pick-me-up," Evie said, raising her chin and blinking back the last of her tears.

Luke nodded, and without hesitation he strode over to Dora and gathered her in his arms. His breath was warm on her ear as he asked, "You doing okay, Dora?"

She was now. Whoa, did his arms feel good around her. She felt the tension she'd been holding ever since she'd followed Sunshine into the enclosure vanish. Sagging against him, she had a flicker of guilt over believing Luke had ditched them once the going got tough. She whispered, "I am now. Did you find out anything?"

"Yes." He pulled away, much to Dora's disappointment, and then lowered his voice as he added, "Billy's in there. But we need to wait until later to get in. Let's get you two back to my place where you can clean up, and then we'll come back to stake out the place until we see an opening. What do you say?"

Dora swayed on her feet, the lack of sleep and stress finally overwhelming her. As much as she didn't want to leave the gator park knowing that Billy was being held inside, she just couldn't see how passing out from exhaustion would help anyone. "Okay. Can I borrow a pillow for a few hours?"

"Me, too," Evie said, rubbing at her red eyes.

He let out a low chuckle. "Two gorgeous women, both asking to use my pillow. You think I'm going to say no to that? In fact, I'll do you one better. How about you both make use of my bed, and I'll rustle up something for lunch?"

"Hero," Dora whispered and gave him a small smile. Just the thought of a nap had turned her into a walking zombie, and without another word, she climbed into Luke's sedan, rested her head against the window, and promptly fell into a fitful sleep.

17

D ora woke with a start. A sound from outside the bedroom had her on edge and she strained to listen, her heart pounding against her breast bone.

"What is it?" a sleepy Evie said from beside her.

They were lying on Luke's bed, where he'd deposited them after they'd bathed Sunshine and showered off the stink of the alligator enclosure. "Nothing," Dora said, patting her friend on the shoulder. "I probably just heard Luke milling around in the kitchen. Go back to sleep."

Evie mumbled something and tightened her arm around Sunshine. Within moments her breathing had deepened, and Dora knew she'd fallen back to sleep.

Dora got up, anxious to talk to Luke about what he'd seen at the gator park. She found a clean T-shirt and jeans in the bag of clothes they'd purchased at Target and made her way down to the kitchen to find Luke.

He was sitting at his kitchen bar, his pen gliding over a piece of paper. She shoved her hands into her pockets and said, "Hey."

His head jerked up as if she'd startled him, but a small smile claimed his lips. "Hey, sleepyhead. Did you get enough rest?"

Dora shrugged. "I don't know. Coffee would be good, though."

He popped off his stool and headed straight for his cappuccino machine. "Have a seat. I'll have this right up and then I'll heat up something to eat for you."

Dora sat on the stool next to his and rubbed her eyes. It had been a heck of a couple of days. Her vision was blurry after she pulled her hands away, and she blinked rapidly, trying to focus on the paper he'd been doodling on. The cappuccino machine buzzed, and she picked up the paper and waved it at him. "What's this?"

"A map of the alligator park. I figured Evie and you'd both want to understand where we're headed when we break in to get Billy tonight. It'll be good to know where all of the exits are."

"You seem... experienced at this kind of thing," Dora said not sure if she was serious or teasing. "Have you rescued a mailman from an abduction before, Luke Landucci?"

He snorted. "Hardly. My specialty is in rescuing damsels in distress. Especially really gorgeous ones who insist on using me for my bed."

Dora laughed for what felt like the first time since before that gun had accidentally gone off. "Thanks. But you probably need an eye exam if you're calling me gorgeous." She'd meant her comment to be lighthearted and self-deprecating, but Luke's grin fled as his eyes darkened with something that looked an awful lot like irritation. "I mean—"

"Don't do that, Dora," he said softly, making his way back over to her with the cappuccino in his hand. "You are gorgeous. I mean, look at you. Tall, curves in all the right places, shiny dark hair, and full pink lips that... um." He cleared his throat. "Anyway. My comment was a compliment. I wish you'd just accept it and say thank you."

Dora swallowed, rather impressed and a bit curious about

his assessment of her. Like he'd given it some thought. And that had her thinking... She nodded. "Thank you."

"There. That wasn't so hard, was it?" He grinned at her and handed her the mug of cappuccino.

She watched him walk back into the kitchen and had to fight to keep from whispering, *yes*. It wasn't everyday a man complimented her. That was more Evie's lane. Just accepting it graciously was something Dora would have to work on. But since she and Evie would be leaving town, it wasn't something she'd have to get used to soon. She eyed the paper, studying it. "You're a pretty good artist."

"Thanks." He pulled a bowl out of the refrigerator and popped it into the microwave. "Is it clear? Can you tell what the room looks like?"

Dora stared down at the paper, and almost chuckled. How could she not. It was so detailed he'd even drawn a likeness of Billy tied to a stool inside a plastic diver's cage. But as soon as she locked her eyes on Billy's hopeless expression, all traces of humor died in the back of her throat. "He looks so... like he's given up."

The microwave beeped and Luke removed the dish, placing it in front of her with a fork and napkin. "He's been there for almost twenty-four hours now, Dora. I'm sure he's exhausted."

"I know. I just feel... this wouldn't be happening if I hadn't dragged everyone into it. He'd be home, watching a football game or Jeopardy. Instead, he's going to be gator food."

Luke clasped his hand over hers. "Not if I can help it. We'll get him out tonight. One way or another. That's a promise, Dora."

"Thank you." She stared down at the bowl of pasta he'd set before her. It looked and smelled a lot like fettuccini in a lemon, cream and garlic sauce, a recipe of Luke's she'd sampled before. It should have made her salivate in anticipation of the mouthwatering flavor, but her stomach was so jumpy she wasn't sure it was wise to try it.

"Eat," he ordered. "You need your strength."

Not wanting to offend him or appear rude after he'd gone to the trouble to make her pasta, she scooped up a forkful and shoved it into her mouth. Then she closed her eyes and moaned as the combination of cream, lemon and garlic exceeded her expectations. "Oh, Luke. This is wonderful."

When she opened her eyes, he was grinning and said, "I remembered how much you liked it. It's foolproof way to get you to moan."

In case Dora didn't get his double entendre, he winked. And it was all she could do to nod her agreement. She dipped her head to hide her flaming cheeks and focus on eating more, forgetting all about her jumpy stomach.

He sat beside her. "How well do you know your neighbor, Brian?"

Dora stopped eating, and her fork hovered in midair as she answered. "A few days ago, I'd have said pretty well. He is my neighbor after all. But now?" She shrugged. "I have no idea. I always thought he was one of the good guys, but it's clear he isn't. I guess I'm easy to fool." She slid pasta off her fork with her teeth to eat it.

Luke turned to eye her. "You're no fool, Dora. If you were, you'd already be in custody."

She swallowed her mouthful of food. "Thanks for that, but I think it's sheer dumb luck."

"You have your theories and I have mine," he said kindly. His brows knit together as he studied the map he'd made. "I just don't get it. What makes a guy like that get into bed with money launderers?"

"I'd imagine he's getting a cut of the profits," Dora said.

Luke turned to her. "That's what I would've thought, too, but doesn't he drive a ten-year-old car and live in his grandmother's house?"

"Yeah." Dora put the fork down and blinked at him. "He also does all the home repairs and yard work. And on his days off, he wears blue jeans and T-shirts."

Luke nodded. "Not the lifestyle of a guy with plenty of money, is it?"

Dora thought back to Steve and Marco. Those two always wore suits, picked up a new lease on a luxury vehicle every two years, and weren't shy about flaunting their money. "Nope. Not the ones I know."

"It doesn't make any sense." Luke shrugged. "Not unless he's being blackmailed."

Dora blew out a breath and shook her head. "Maybe he's socking it all away for a mail order bride or plans to buy a small island once his criminal days are behind him." She scooped up another forkful of pasta. "Or maybe he's smart and making sure he appears as someone who lives on a cop's salary."

"All possibilities. But something about him isn't quite adding up. What makes a cop turn shady, and why didn't he just take you to Marco right away if he's in so deep with the Franklins' operation?"

"Because he wanted the evidence," Dora reasoned.

"He could've gotten that without you," Luke said.

He had a point. Brian could've gotten a warrant to get the information off the computers himself. "Okay. Say that's true. Maybe he just likes me and didn't want me to come to any harm."

Luke raised one eyebrow. "Dora. He's a cop. He knows how dangerous it is to let you roam around with the knowledge you have. Any reasonable criminal would've had you in front of Marco as soon as possible."

"I don't know. Maybe he just has more of a conscience than

the rest of them. He did sign up to be a cop after all." Dora sighed. She knew what she was saying didn't make sense, and something was niggling at her when it came to Brian. She recalled he mentioned someone named Morris when they overheard him at the dry cleaners. But she hadn't had enough sleep in the past two days to make sense of it, and her brain was starting to hurt.

Luke put a warm hand on her shoulder. "I know you like, or *did* like him, but I think there's more to him than meets the eye. It doesn't hurt to remain curious, right?"

"Right." Dora pushed her almost empty pasta bowl away as the urgency to *do something* hit her, and she got to her feet. "I'm going to wake Evie. We have a mailman to save."

"I'll make her and Sunshine something to eat," Luke said, and he pressed a soft kiss to her temple.

Dora's stomach flipped at the gesture, making her feel like a teenager again, and she was sure her lips were curved into a small, happy smile as she climbed the stairs.

18

"Luke's right," Evie said, finishing off her own bowl of pasta. "Brian is definitely up to something more than just trying to protect the Franklins. Look at him. He appears to be about two more beers away from homelessness. That's not the way a man who is laundering money looks."

"How would you know?" Dora asked as Luke took Evie's dish away.

"I know people," Evie said defensively.

"Sure, Evie," Dora said. "I still say he could be really good at this and just be making it *seem* like he doesn't have any money. He did a great job of making me think he was a nice guy."

Evie choose to ignore her flippant attitude. Dora hated to be wrong, and this whole situation was pushing that button big time for her friend. Besides, nobody likes to think they trusted the wrong person.

There was something else about Brian she'd just remembered. Something he had said a week ago when she'd run into him over at Dora's that had stuck with her. He'd complained about people interfering with their elderly relatives' finances and how disrespectful they were. He'd been so angry

Evie had thought he might pop a vein. It was the type of anger that made a person lose control. Evie had been super anxious in his presence, and all she'd wanted to do was change the subject.

But when she'd asked him if he was a volunteer at a senior living place, he'd barked that his grandfather was at one and then stalked off muttering something about how they were going to be surprised when they'd been cut out of the will. At the time, she'd thought he'd just been rambling, but what if it was something more? Had his grandfather been taken in some old folk's home scam? And if so, did it have something to do with the Franklins?

"Earth to Evie," Dora said, snapping her out of her trance. "We've got to go. Get Sunshine and get your butt in the car. It's time for Operation Rescue Billy."

"Right." Evie let out a soft whistle and called, "Come here, Sunshine. It's time for the next step in Operation Save Dora's Ass."

"Hey," Dora said.

"Yeah?" Evie looked up from the map Luke had drawn.

"Thanks."

The word was spoken simply and clearly, but that didn't stop Evie from cupping her hand behind her ear and saying, "What was that, Dora? Did I just hear you say *thanks*?"

"Stop." Dora rolled her eyes. "You know that's what I said. You heard me the first time."

Evie blew her a kiss as she walked out Luke's front door and headed for his car. "Sunshine calls shotgun!" she cried out, trying and failing to put it out of her mind that they were about to break into the alligator park... again. She glanced down at Sunshine and added, "Be good this time, girl."

Once they were in the car, Evie glanced over at Luke and back at Dora. She blew out a big breath. "We're doing this, team. Got it?" she asked, more to pump herself up than anyone else.

Her stomach was jittery, and it wasn't because the pasta she'd eaten was bad. *Oh man, so not bad*, Evie thought as she recalled the flavor that made her mouth water just thinking about it.

Once they'd hit the road, Dora scooted forward on her seat to insert herself between Luke and Evie. "Do either of you know somebody named Morris?"

Evie searched her brain, and amazingly couldn't come up with one person she knew who had that name. And she knew *a lot* of people. Although... "There was a guy in high school who had Morris as a middle name," she offered. "We teased him so bad. He was the craziest runner, all arms and knees, and one day someone called him Chicken Morrister. It stuck and he was known at Chick Morrister for the rest of the year. Aren't kids awful?" She knew it wasn't helpful, but it was all she had. And Dora was strung so tight right now she needed to lighten the mood.

Luke chuckled. "All I've got is a cat. One of my cooks adopted a cat named Miss Morris. Apparently, the old lady who'd had her thought it was a boy and named it Morris, but then she found out it was a girl."

"So, she added the Miss," Evie said. "Clever."

"How do people not know how to tell the sex of a cat?" Dora asked. "It can't be that complicated."

Luke turned his head to her. "You'd think, but it definitely happens a lot with shelter animals," Luke said.

"Right," Evie piped in. "Once they snip those tiny man parts off it's hard to tell." Evie let out a small gasp. "Wait. An old lady owned Miss Morris?"

"It's sad," Luke said. "The woman died of a sudden heart attack, and her cat was left behind."

"Oh my god!" Evie said, recalling her half-baked idea that Brian might be involved in a senior citizen scam. Only maybe the person that had been taken advantage of wasn't *his* relative.

Maybe it was Miss Morris's mistress and Brian was behind the scam. "Was she in a home for old folks by any chance?"

"Assisted living," Dora corrected.

"She was. Riverwoods. Have you seen the place?" Luke let out a low whistle. "It's like a resort. I'll tell you, whoever runs that joint has it figured out. The residents have so much money they play shuffleboard with golden pucks."

"The perfect place to run a scam, wouldn't you say?" Evie asked.

"Wow," Dora said. "You guys, this may be a long shot, but when Sunshine managed to turn on the audio of the surveillance camera at the dry cleaners, we got the tail end of a sentence. Remember, Evie?"

Evie shrugged because what she remembered was how proud she'd been of Sunshine. That little dog really took her yoga seriously.

Dora said, "We heard him say, *Miss Morris*. I thought Brian mentioned someone named Morris, but what if he was referring to a cat?"

"Dora!" Evie cried, suddenly remembering the conversation they'd eavesdropped on. "The next thing we heard was Jock saying animal cruelty wasn't in the contract. Do you think Brian had something to do with the woman's death and Jock insisted on bringing the cat to a shelter? Crap!"

"That's not as far-fetched as you'd think," Luke said. "The girl who works for me also works part-time at Riverwoods, and that's where she got the cat."

Evie glanced back at Dora whose eyes were wide open.

"See?" Dora said. "Maybe Brian is in on a scam and just dresses down."

Evie chuckled and let Dora be right. "I guess so. What do we do about it?"

Dora sighed. "I don't know. I mean, this could just be our

imaginations putting together random bits of information because humans love correlations."

"This is why she's an accountant," Luke said. Evie noticed he was smiling with pride. That man was definitely someone Dora needed in her life. But first they needed to salvage said life. And the first step was to rescue Billy.

"Whatever." Evie rolled her eyes, because Dora's need for logic could get super annoying. They were just down the street from the alligator park, and Luke slowed his car and snapped off the lights. Evie whispered as if someone could hear through the car's exterior. "Don't want to alert anyone to our arrival."

"Smart," Dora whispered with what Evie suspected was sarcasm.

Lack of sleep and high stress levels were making the best friends cranky with each other, and Evie didn't like it. Once Luke stopped the car she turned to Dora in the back seat. "Hey, if we're going to get through this, we need to be our best selves. Okay?"

"Sorry." Dora held out her pinky and Evie hooked onto it with her own tiny digit. "BFFs 4E."

Evie smiled at their long-standing joke. When they were young, Evie didn't know that BFF already had forever in it and added the 4 and the E. So technically, they were saying best friends forever four ever. But even after Evie learned her mistake it had stuck. "BFF's4E."

Luke said, "Ladies, are we ready for this?"

Evie and Dora gazed into each other's eyes with determination, and in unison they said, "Let's do it."

19

"Ugh," Dora said as she tried not to breathe through her nose. The three of them were tiptoeing with Luke in the lead to the back of the alligator park to access a service entrance. This time Sunshine was secured in a baby backpack Luke had snagged from another neighbor who was away. That man had a lot of keys to other people's homes, it seemed, and so many neighbors who clearly trusted him to watch over things while they were gone.

"Right?" Evie asked. "How does anyone work here with that smell?"

"They acclimate," Dora said, annoying even herself by responding since she knew Evie didn't really want an answer. God, she really was a pain sometimes. although she knew she was focusing on facts to stay sane. Her logic had gotten her through most difficulties in her life, and it was hard not to rely on it now. Even if her stupid logic was how she'd ended up in this position in the first place.

They approached a dumpster, which added another disgusting odor to the sickening cocktail they were inhaling, and Luke stopped moving. He held up his hand. He turned, and his eyes shone with the reflection of a streetlight as he whispered, "Let's run over the plan one more time. I'll lead us to Billy because I know exactly where the security cameras are and how to avoid them."

Dora nodded and gave Evie a serious glare. It's not that Evie meant to ruin the best laid plans, but she was known to go off the rails. "You understand this part, right?"

"Yes, Dora," Evie said and then followed up with a huff. "I understand I'm to follow Luke and not get distracted by anything *shiny*."

"Didn't you two just have a pinky-swearing, initial-filled bonding moment where you promised not to be snippy anymore?" Luke asked.

"Sorry, Evie," Dora said.

"It's okay. You're right; I sometimes get distracted. But I won't this time. I promise."

Luke watched the two women for a moment, and when they both gazed at him with a look that said *what are you waiting for?* he continued, "Once we get to Billy, I'm going to distract the alligator that's guarding him."

Luke had shown Evie and Dora his sketch of Billy, who was sitting on a stool inside a large, clear plastic cylinder one might see protecting a human in a big aquarium. It was suspended partway inside a pool of water that housed at least one alligator.

Evie said to him, "You're going to do the distraction this time."

"I am," Luke confirmed.

Dora was glad. She'd had enough of being alligator bait to last a lifetime. "And while you do that, Evie and I find a way to get Billy out of his tank and into your car."

"Good thing I packed a snack for him," Evie said, patting the straps of the baby backpack she was wearing. "He's bound to be starving after all this time in captivity." The pack was made to hold a baby, the part Sunshine was utilizing, but it also had a pocket for other items a parent might need. "Sunshine's guarding them for safekeeping."

The little dog let out a shocked sounding yelp, and Dora took a good look at the pup, noticing brown stains around her furry white snout that looked suspiciously like peanut butter.

The dog curled her upper lip at Dora in silence, warning her not to tell Evie how well the peanut butter bar had actually been guarded. Dora shrugged. She understood that emergency snacks were for a variety of stressful situations, like say, returning to the place where you were almost a doggy truffle for a gator. Besides, it was gone now, and not much could be done about it.

"Then," Dora began, "we get Billy home and swear him to secrecy about us. Since Evie returned the truck and clocked him out as usual—"

Evie cut in, "And we delivered all his mail."

"He returns to work as usual on Monday," Dora finished. They had discussed this previously, but Dora was still uneasy about this portion of their plan. "Jeez, I sure hope he's going to be agreeable to this. What if he wants to go to the police anyway?"

"He delivers Brian's mail, too," Evie said. "Relax, Dora. Billy's not going to trust the police any more than we do considering he knows the one who kidnapped him."

She sighed, knowing Evie was likely right, but it didn't make her queasy stomach feel much better.

Luke said, "Okay. We're good. Now, I need you both to watch my back while I pick the lock."

Dora's jaw dropped. She'd figured they were going to crawl through a window or something. "*You're* going to pick the lock?" she asked.

Luke smiled. "Way too many James Bond movies as a kid. Did you know my favorite cocktail is a martini?"

"Shaken, not stirred," Evie said with a grin, and then she sighed. "It's soooo sexy when a man orders that."

Dora elbowed her friend when a twinge of jealousy stabbed at her heart. "How should we alert you if we see something?" she asked Luke.

"Clear your throat, like this," Evie said, and then she proceeded to make a noise that sounded like she was about to hack up one hell of a loogie.

"Ewww, Evie," Dora said.

"What? It's allergy season and I've been a little too busy to remember to take my medicine. You know how bad my phlegm gets."

"Now that's sexy," Luke said. "Bet that gets you a lot of dates."

"I do just fine, thank you very much, Chef Luke, ye who has access to way too many neighbors' apartments."

"Right?" Dora asked, happy her friend had the same suspicions.

"Apparently, I do just find too," Luke snapped back, catching his error in judgment too late. He looked at Dora. "I mean—" He stammered, and then he shook his head. "I'm not dating any of them. Never have. I'm just the one everyone asks to water their plants and take in mail. I'm a sucker that way."

Dora's heart softened because she loved that he was so trustworthy. "No. You're a nice guy, Luke."

"Great," Evie said. "I'm disgusting, Luke's a nice guy, and Dora's got a mad crush on him. Now that that's settled, let's break into an alligator park and save a mailman. Okay?"

"Fine," Dora said, cheeks burning from embarrassment. "How about a heron call?" She let out a raspy sound similar to one someone might make to mimic a pterodactyl.

"Wow. That's scary good," Luke said.

"Sounds like your loogie got stuck," Evie mumbled.

Dora ignored her friend and smiled at Luke. "You had James Bond. I had Animal Planet."

"Well, all right, ladies." Luke nodded at them and walked quietly over to the service entrance door.

Luke managed to get the door open almost as fast as if he'd had the key, and Dora exchanged a wide-eyed glance with Evie. Evie asked, "Who needs James Bond? We've got Luke."

As she stepped softly through the door, Dora marveled at his skill too. Luke sure was something, and she was really glad he'd offered to help them. She had a feeling Billy would be too.

The inside of the alligator park was creepy at night. The lighting was dim, and along with the chirping of crickets and peeping of frogs, the alligators let out rumbly groans that made tiny hairs stand up on the back of Dora's neck. She shuddered as she recalled she was almost a meal for them earlier. She really hoped rescuing Billy was going to be a quick job.

"How much further?" Evie asked in a loud whisper.

"Almost there." Luke pressed his back up against a wall and shuffled to the side, apparently in an effort to hide from a security camera. Evie, whom Dora had insisted go next so she could keep an eye on her, followed him, and then Dora did the same. They turned a corner, and Luke paused by a door to check the handle. It was locked, but that wasn't much of a problem for Luke, and he let them into the room a few moments later.

"Billy!" Evie hissed.

The man had likely been asleep, because he lifted his head and his back straightened up as if she'd woken him.

"Billy! It's me!" Evie said in her whisper, which was pointless since it was just as loud as a speaking voice.

"Evie? Is that you?" Billy asked.

Evie lurched forward, but Luke grabbed her shirt to restrain her just in time. "Hang on a minute there, sister," he said. "You might want to consider his guard first." Luke pointed to a large, dark object that appeared to be a rock at first, but Dora quickly realized it was an alligator. A really big one. "Meet Cecelia," Luke said. "Fourteen feet of pure gator. And from my research, I learned she's never been one to miss out on the opportunity for a good meal."

"Billy," Evie said, "We're here to rescue you. Just hold tight."

"H—how?" Dora asked as she eyed Cecelia, who had opened one eye to see what was going on. Luke hadn't drawn her to size. *At all.* Or mentioned the part where there wasn't a partition or any sort of divider to keep the alligator from attacking them.

Dora looked at Luke and whispered, "Don't you think it might have been a good idea to tell us about Cecelia, *Mr. Bond*?"

20

"I've always had a little trouble with scale when it comes to sketching," Luke said.

"Ya think?" Evie asked. Luke had made the alligator that was guarding Billy seem like something he could easily handle. Evie had to admit that Luke had been pretty competent so far. Waiting all night to rescue her and Dora from the dry cleaners was admirable. Figuring out how to get inside the alligator park and bypassing the cameras was darn clever, too. But she wasn't so sure the James Bond wannabe could safely distract a fourteen-foot gator. "Someone's been spending a little too much time inhaling whipped cream in the walk-in cooler at work."

"For Pete's sake, you two," Luke said. Then he glared at Evie. "Wait a minute, that was you?" He shook his head as he let out a sigh. "And to think, I blamed the dishwasher for doing the whipits to get high. I knew there was more to the story about the bartender having a run on orange wedges."

"Hey!" Evie said. She may have partaken in a little nitrous oxide fun *with* the dishwasher during her two-week stint as a waitress at Luke's restaurant, but now was not the time to admit it. "Don't we have a man to save here?"

"Yeah," piped in Billy. "I'd really like to get back in time for the football game. I've got money ridin' on the Dolphins."

Dora shook her head and kicked off her shoes. Evie knew her friend was also skeptical about Luke's gator-taming abilities, but she knew Dora would do anything to try to rescue Billy anyway.

"How do we want to do this?" Dora asked.

"Give me a minute to deal with Cecelia," Luke said. "I'll hold up my thumb when you're good to go."

"Like you're hitchhiking?" Dora asked.

Luke frowned. "No. Like a thumbs-up." He demonstrated by lifting his thumb and extending it straight up. "Like, this. You know? The universal everything's-okay sign."

"Is that what that means?" Evie asked in a joking tone as she recalled what Dora had thought it meant the first time someone used it on her. "I thought that was more of a *Hey, babe, wanna get with me later?* kind of sign. Right, Dor?"

"Funny," Dora said. She pointed her thumbs up and her index fingers out to mimic guns and clicked twice. "*That's* the do-me-later sign."

Evie tried to hide her snicker. Try as she might, there were just some things Dora was never going to get.

"What? You—I—" Luke shook his head, completely dumbfounded.

Evie laughed. "You don't want to know what she thought the middle finger was for."

"Hey! I was a new driver. How was I supposed to know the guy wasn't trying to tell me to get in the middle lane?"

Luke let out a snort of laughter. Evie joined him, and even Billy grinned at Dora's expense.

Dora, however, was not so entertained. She crossed her arms and glared at Evie. "You sure you really want to start this?"

Evie found a way to stop laughing and held up a hand. She knew Dora had some darn good dirt on her too, and she did not want to go there. "No. I'm sorry."

Luke managed to stop laughing too, and as he wiped his eyes, he said, "Dora, you're are so damn cute sometimes."

"Great. Another person in my life who likes to laugh at my expense."

Luke reached out to put a hand on one of Dora's crossed arms. "No, babe. I mean it. I like this side of you. It's adorable and refreshing."

Dora's expression softened, and she dipped her head to give him a sideways glance. "Oh. Okay, then."

Billy cleared his throat loudly. "Any chance I can make the second half?"

"Right." Luke straightened up and took a deep breath before he began to walk slowly over to Cecelia. The alligator was clearly not laughing when she opened her wide jaw to reveal her bone-crushing teeth. The gator let out low growl that chilled Evie to the bone.

It didn't do much to affect Luke, though. He stopped a few feet from the gator and began to sing softly, starting off with a long croon of her name. The lyrics went on to say she was breaking Luke's heart.

Evie's jaw dropped in surprise, and it wasn't because Luke knew the words to the classic tune. She turned to look at Dora to find she'd had the same reaction. "He's singing to her?"

Dora continued to stare, mesmerized. "Uh-huh."

Evie understood why. Luke had the voice of an angel. Well, not quite as good as Trace's but, damn, not too shabby. And with the cement walls in the room they were in, the acoustics were doing him a huge favor. Luke sloshed slowly into the water to get closer to Cecelia as he sang.

Not only was Dora awestruck and Evie impressed, but Cecelia had closed her mouth, and she slithered closer to Luke to rub against him like she was a cat looking for affection. Even Sunshine was leaning her head on Evie's shoulder, watching as if she was transfixed by Luke's song. They were all so mesmerized nobody seemed to notice when Luke lifted up his thumb.

"Pssst!" Billy said. "A little help here?"

Evie snapped out of her trance. "Coming. Coming." She grabbed her friend's arm. "Dor! C'mon."

"Right." Dora shook her head and rushed over with Evie to help Billy out of his tank. The two women found it wasn't difficult. Apparently, Brian and Jock had felt that Cecelia was enough of a deterrent that they didn't need to tie Billy up too tight. Plus, Dora had a box cutter in her back pocket that helped make quick work of removing the duct tape holding Billy to his stool.

By the time they got Billy out of the tank and on solid ground again, Cecelia had rolled onto her back in the knee-deep water, and Luke was rubbing her stomach as he continued to sing. He'd moved her back into the shadows, and his voice was so soft Evie guessed Cecelia must be asleep.

"Unbelievable," Billy said.

"It really is," Evie agreed. "I've never—" She let out a gasp, and Sunshine yelped as something hard was jammed into Evie's side.

"Ladies," Brian said. Evie noticed he had an arm around Dora's neck and a gun in her side. "How nice of you to drop by."

"Crap," Dora mumbled.

"Aw, man," Billy whined. "Hey, do either of you guys know who's winning the Dolphins game?"

"Twenty-one to nine. Dol—"

"Jock!" Brian shouted. He waved his gun toward Billy. "Back in your tank or the girl joins you."

"If you're going to put one of them in there with me, can it be Evie?" Billy winked at Evie and darted his eyes toward where Cecelia was resting sans Luke.

Evie frowned, pretending she was insulted, and snuck a glance over at the gator to see Luke wasn't anywhere in sight. She figured Billy was buying them some time.

Billy shrugged as he looked at her, playing his part to the hilt. At least she hoped so, because he said, "I mean, if I get to choose. 'Cause Evie's kind of hot. She answers the door in short-shorts and those little tank tops some girls wear. You know?" He glanced at Dora. "I'm sure you're hot too, but you wear way more clothes. No offense."

"None taken," Dora said. And Evie believed Dora meant it and was on board with their ruse.

"*Kind* of hot?" Evie asked in an exasperated voice. She let it rise in volume. "I'm only *kind* of hot?"

"I don't know," Jock said from behind Evie. "Dora's got a little something, something going on, too."

Dora opened her mouth in shock, and Evie didn't think she was acting. "I—I'm—"

"Hot, Dora," Evie said. "Jock thinks you're hot. See?"

"For crying out loud!" Brian yelled. "Will you people shut up?"

"Jeez," Evie said. "You could have asked nic—"

Brian's tone got nastier. "Zip it!"

Jock whispered to Evie. "Too much caffeine makes him cranky."

"That," Brian snapped, "and women who think they're too smart for their own good." He looked at Billy. "Get in the damn tank."

"Okay, but who—"

"Alone!"

Billy jumped, and so did Evie, Dora, Jock and Brian. But not because Brian yelled. Cecelia let out a low growl, and when Evie turned to look at the gator, she saw the reptile was on the move. Sunshine yelped, and Brian and Jock both shoved their hostages in front of themselves to offer up bait for the gator.

"Coward," Evie said just before she yelled to Dora, "The old one-two!" Dora might have been horrible with hand signals but bark out an order and she'd hop to it. Evie was taking a chance, but a good one, because she knew that Brian needed her and Dora alive to locate the flash drive. The old one-two was a self-defense move they'd learned in a class together. And she knew Dora practiced it regularly.

Evie lifted her foot and stomped on Jock's arch as hard as she could. He grunted in pain and loosened his grip enough that she was able to twist around and knee him hard. Right where it counted. Jock doubled over in pain as Evie grabbed his weapon to train it on him. She heard Brian's cries and glanced over at Dora.

Brian was rolling on the ground, groaning as Dora scrambled after the gun that he'd dropped. She looked at Evie with wide eyes. "Whoa. It worked."

"Of course it did," Evie said, feeling her lips split into a self-satisfied smile as she pressed her heel on one of Jock's wrists just to make him groan. *Serves him right,* she thought as she increased the pressure, knowing it was wrong to enjoy torturing him so much, but she didn't exactly care. These bastards had tried to kill Billy. "We're badass. Remember that."

Cecelia slithered closer to the men with Luke by her side. He was dripping wet from head to toe, making Evie think he'd hidden under Cecelia until the time was right.

"Not that badass," Brian growled, rolling up onto his feet and lunging for Dora.

"Dora, look out!" Evie cried, rushing Brian to save her friend. But she was too far away. Instead, Sunshine shot forward and sank her teeth into Brian's ankle, distracting him just enough that Dora was able to grab his arm, twist it behind his back, and yank up hard, bringing him to his knees.

"What is your problem, Brian?" Dora said with an angry sneer. "Here I thought you were my friend, and instead you tied me and Evie up in the dry cleaners, and now you're involved in a plan to murder Billy? What happened to you?"

"Get off me, Dora, or when I bring you in, your charges are going to include assaulting a police officer," he said.

Dora snorted. "You're not bringing anyone in, Brian. Look at you and your sidekick. Neither one of you have control of this situation."

Evie let out a giggle and felt pride swell in her chest. Watching her friend go all kickass on the cop was insane, but Evie approved. He was a jerk of huge proportions. "Come here, Sunshine," Evie said. "Good girl. You helped Auntie Dora restrain Brian over there."

Sunshine let out a happy bark and ran over to Evie, plopping down right at her feet.

"She really is something," Jock agreed.

Evie glanced down at him where he lay. He was staring at Cecilia, and Evie knew he was behaving because the gator was within striking distance. If she hadn't seen Luke controlling the gator with her own two eyes, she might've been concerned with her own proximity to the beast. But Luke definitely had her under control. She grinned down at Jock. "Right?"

Brian struggled against Dora's hold. "Let go of me, or I'm going to make this really difficult for you, Dora."

"I don't think so. Why don't you tell me how you got involved with the Franklins and why you're so willing to turn a blind eye to their money laundering?" Dora said, yanking on his arm again.

He let out a hiss. "You bitc—"

"Don't you dare say that to my friend," Evie said with a low growl. "Besides, how unoriginal can you get?" She cast a glance at Jock, who was still staring at the gator beside Luke. Certain that Luke didn't need her to guard Jock, she crossed the room to stand right behind Dora. "What are your secrets, Brian? And what's your connection to Riverwoods?"

His eyes widened in surprise before he scowled at her. "What do you know?"

"Ah-ha! Jackpot. You are running some kind of scam over there, aren't you? And the Franklins are helping you hide the money, right?" Evie demanded.

"Evie!" Dora said, jabbing her in the gut with an elbow. "Not now."

"If not now, when? We have to figure out why he's disgracing his badge. What better time than the present while that gator over there contemplates chowing down on his nuts."

Brian let out a whimper.

Evie laughed. "We have him right where we want him."

"Wrong," a strange voice called from behind them. "Let the officer go, Dora, and we might let you live."

Ice ran through Evie's veins as she recognized the voice.

"Marco?" Evie asked as he stepped out of the shadows.

"Making sure nothing happens to my investments." He pulled out a nine-millimeter and pointed it right at Dora. "Release the cop. Now."

Dora visibly swallowed, and her hands started to shake.

Evie's head began to spin as she frantically tried to rack her brain for how to get out of this situation. She believed Marco would have no trouble killing the woman who'd killed his father. They were royally screwed.

"Do it!" Marco barked, waving the gun wildly.

Sunshine let out a whimper as she cowered at Evie's feet. She longed to bend down and scoop up her scared pup, but she didn't dare move. Dora let go of Brian and started to back up.

Brian twisted, grabbing Dora just as Cecilia lunged for him, and Evie let out a blood-curdling scream.

21

Pain radiated up Dora's arm, making her stomach turn. She let out a loud gasp and tried to jerk back, but the intense pain sent her straight to her knees. Pure rage had her seeing red, and on instinct she'd carefully cultivated with daily practice, she used her free arm and jabbed her fingers right into Brian's eyes.

They were softer than she'd expected, and the wetness of his eyes made her stomach turn, but he dropped his hold on her and she quickly scrambled back up just in time for Cecilia to shoot past her, jaws open as she lunged for Brian.

"Let's go," Luke said into her ear.

The sound of his calming voice washed over Dora, and she turned to him with her eyes wide. "The gator—"

"She's doing exactly what I told her to do. She won't kill him. She'll just keep him detained for a while," he said and tugged her away from the cop and the beast.

Dora couldn't bring herself to turn and look at the scene behind her. Instead, she frantically scanned the area for Evie and Sunshine, and was relieved to find them already hurrying out of the room with Billy right behind them.

Someone moaned off the to the right, and when she glanced over, she spotted Marco writhing on the ground, his arm cradled to his chest and no gun in sight.

"Did you take him down?" she asked Luke.

"We can thank my martial arts training for that." He gave her an encouraging smile. "Let's go."

At least that was something. She sped up and darted out of the room too, hoping she never saw another alligator again. It was a stretch considering she lived in Florida, but a girl could dream, right?

With no need to worry about the security cameras now, Luke and she rushed down the hall and through the gator park toward the exit. Bullets rang out behind them, followed by shouts and orders for them to stop. Dora was nearly paralyzed by fear, but Luke grabbed her wrist and pulled her into the shadows as he continued to jog and hissed, "Just keep moving."

Without any other plan of action, she did as he said and prayed Evie and Sunshine would be all right.

"This way." Luke came to a sudden stop before he pushed through an emergency exit. More bullets blasted behind them, and she wondered if they were still aiming at them, or...

"Evie," she whispered with her hand to her throat.

Luke grabbed her arm and, stepping behind her, practically pushed her through the gate. "Just keep moving. They're fine, understand?"

She nodded, her heart in her throat. *How did I get myself into this mess?* she wondered for the thousandth time.

Relief washed over Dora when Evie called out, "Over here!" She was waving frantically for them beside Luke's car. Evie slipped into the driver's seat. Sunshine hopped in after her, while Billy climbed into the back seat.

Dora took off at a dead run, no longer unsure of her next move. She sprinted so fast she was sure if she were in a race she'd have broken some sort of record. Before she knew it, she was crammed in the back seat of the car with Billy.

Once Luke was safely in the car as well, Evie peeled out, more than likely leaving rubber on the road.

Billy leaned his head against Dora's shoulder. "I'm starving," He said.

Dora wrapped her arms around him and held on. "Evie. Your purse?"

"You know it, Dor."

"I have food at my house. Just go straight there," Luke said.

"But Evie has Poptarts," Dora said. "Blueberry ones."

"Blueberry?" Billy asked.

"That is not food." Luke shook his head but retrieved the toaster pastries from Evie's purse. He turned and handed the treat to Billy as he eyed Dora. "We seriously have to discuss what constitutes a meal when this is all done."

When this is done? "Right," Dora said, trying and failing to contain her giddy smile. She gently ran a hand over Billy's back, trying to give him some comfort and to focus on the seriousness of what had just happened.

Billy let out a small moan as he devoured the sugary junk food. "That was some serious alligator whispering," he forced out. "Thanks for saving my tush."

Luke reached back and squeezed the man's hand. "No way were we going to leave you there, Billy. Don't worry. We've got it from here."

Billy nodded and let out a deep sigh as he leaned his head on the window and closed his eyes.

Dora met Luke's gaze. The two stared at each other for a long moment, and she wondered what he was thinking. She'd panicked back there, and if Luke hadn't grabbed her, she might have been shot while frozen in fear. She said, "Thank you, Luke. I don't know what we would've done without you."

He gave her a hint of a smile. "I'm betting you and Evie would've figured something out. I'm picturing paintball guns and ski masks. But I was glad to help."

Evie let out a snort. "I'm gonna need to stock my purse with paintball guns *and* Poptarts now. That's a great idea."

"Aren't you even the least bit freaked out?" Dora demanded. She glanced between the two of them. "We were just shot at, And Billy was almost gator food!"

Luke turned again, but instead of saying anything, this time he reached back and grabbed Dora's hand, squeezing it tightly.

Evie took a sharp turn down a side street. "Nah, Dora. They weren't shooting at us. They were shooting at each other. I don't know what was going down, but Marco seemed pissed at Brian and Jock. Maybe they messed up the job so bad Marco was ready to be done with them. Either way, we've got Billy, and now we can start making plans to find the evidence we need to clear you."

Dora slumped back into her seat. She didn't think Evie and Luke were taking the situation as seriously as they should. She wished it were true that Evie and she could leave Luke and Billy to deal with any fallout while they hightailed it to New Orleans to retrieve the flash drive, but didn't they need to make sure the two weren't in any danger first? Dora pressed her fingers to her temples and tried not to let her anxiety get the best of her.

"Don't stress, Dora," Evie said almost cheerily. "We've got this. You'll see."

"Famous last words," Dora muttered and pressed her head to the cool glass of her window.

Evie just chuckled. "Always the pessimist."

Dora preferred to think of herself as logical, but she knew that sometimes she could be pessimistic, too. But at the moment, she couldn't imagine feeling any other way.

DORA SWIRLED her frothy cappuccino remains in her cup as she said, "I don't think it's wise that we keep coming back here." They were sitting at Luke's kitchen table while he cooked.

"Where else are we going to go?" Evie asked.

Dora knew she was right, but it didn't make her any less nervous.

"Besides," Evie added. "We're out of here in the morning. That should turn the heat down considerably."

"We can't just leave Billy and Luke as sitting ducks," Dora insisted. "Do you really think Brian and Marco are going to just stop looking for us? Besides, the minute Billy goes home, they'll be pounding his door down."

Evie frowned and bit on her bottom lip as she petted Sunshine. The dog was curled up in her lap, staying as close to her mother as possible. It appeared the gunshots had rattled at least one other soul besides Dora. "So, what is it you think we should do? We can't go to the cops. We don't know who's dirty and who isn't."

"True." Dora tapped her fingers against her lips and glanced over at Luke, who was busy making food again. He'd already supplied Billy with water and some truffle cheese. Because doesn't everyone have that in their fridge? Now he was working on a late-night dinner for all of them. The heavenly scent of onions and garlic wafted over her, and her mouth started to water. Luke was right, Poptarts were so not a meal you had with him around.

"Earth to Dora." Evie waved her hands in front of her friend's face. "Focus, will you? You can drool over the hottie in the kitchen later."

Luke glanced over his shoulder at Dora, giving her a knowing grin. Dora's face flushed, and she thought she might die right there on the spot. "Thanks a lot, Evie," she whispered through clenched teeth.

"Pshaw." Evie rolled her eyes. "You two are so hot for each other I'm about to get heat exhaustion just being in your presence. Don't act like it's not happening. None of us are stupid."

Luke let out a low chuckle but didn't turn back around.

Dora sucked in a deep breath and closed her eyes. "This isn't the time for this conversation. Let's get back to working out a plan."

Evie sat back in her chair. "We don't have a plan."

Dora ignored her painfully obvious statement. "We need to expose Brian. Figure out what his deal is, so that the heat is on him and not us. I think we should head to Riverwoods and find out why exactly he spends so much time there. He's already inadvertently confirmed that something is up."

"Do we know anyone who works there?" Evie asked as Billy's gaze bounced back and forth between the two women.

Dora turned her attention to Luke. "You said a cook you know adopted Miss Morris, right? How did that happen? Did she get her from a shelter, or did she just take her from Riverwoods after her owner died?"

"Hmm." Luke started placing his steak stir fry onto four plates. "Cassie didn't say. I can give her a call."

Cassie. Dora knew it was irrational, but she suddenly had a vague mental picture of Luke laughing and flirting with another woman... one who shared his passion for cooking.

"You do that," Evie said, setting Sunshine on the floor. "I'm going to call Trace and see if he knows anyone." She slid out of her chair and disappeared into the next room.

Luke glanced at the clock. "It's a little late to call Cassie. I think I should wait until the morning."

Billy piped in. "I know who delivers the mail at Riverwoods.

Kyle Johnson. Want me to call him? Feel him out for what he knows?"

Dora didn't like the idea of bringing Billy any further into the situation. Besides which, she wasn't sure his friend would have any useful information as a mailman. She reached over and touched Billy's arm. "That's sweet, but I think one kidnapped mailman is all my conscience can handle."

Billy placed his hand on hers. "Sure. But I have another way I can help. Jock and Brian weren't exactly worried about the things I heard."

Maybe the caffeine of her cappuccino had just kicked in, or maybe it was because Luke set food down before Dora, but she perked up and said, "Tell us more."

22

Evie listened to Trace's voicemail message for the third time. She didn't actually think he knew anyone who either worked or lived at Riverwoods. And she knew he was likely still on the stage of whatever gig the band had that night, but she wanted to hear his voice.

The showdown at the alligator park had shaken her up more than she cared to admit. But when they were driving away from the scene, she'd known Dora was one gasp away from falling apart, and Evie had managed to stay strong for her friend. But now she could see that Dora was compensating for the trauma by jumping into action, and it was time for Evie to catch her breath.

Her body began to shake with the delayed shock, and she wrapped her arms around herself. She hadn't signed up for kidnappings and bullets flying. Not that she would change anything she'd done to help Dora.

Dora was her best friend and she'd walk through fire to get her out of a jam. But this was starting to get intense. More intense than Evie had bargained for. Evie lay back down on the bed, staring at the ceiling. She knew Dora was right. They couldn't just leave Luke and Billy hanging in the wind while they took off to New Orleans.

And what about Trace? It wasn't a secret that Evie was involved with him. Would Brian and his criminal friends go after him in order to get to her and Dora? It was more than probable. Her heart stopped for a moment before it filled with so much emotion for her sexy boyfriend that she thought it might burst. She picked up her phone and sent Trace a text. *Miss you. Call when your gig is done. Doesn't matter how late.*

It was only a few minutes later when the phone rang, but Evie had already imagined a shallow grave full of the bodies of her friends. Her heart lurched when she saw Trace's name pop up on her phone. She answered and said, "Hey, baby. Did you have a good crowd?"

"What's wrong?" he asked, his voice full of concern.

"What makes you think there's anything wrong?" she asked, wondering if he'd heard something. Had they already started looking for him? Her insides went cold, and she sat straight up on the bed.

"Evie, you don't ever call me during a gig. And you sure as hell don't ever call multiple times and not leave me messages."

That was true. She loved teasing him and leaving dirty little messages on his phone when he was too busy to talk to her. She couldn't even the remember the last time she'd called and hadn't told him exactly what she wanted when he got back in town. "Fair enough." She let out a deep sigh. "Do you know anyone associated with Riverwoods?"

"The assisted living place on the north end of town?" he asked, sounding confused.

"Yeah. That's the one."

There was silence on the other end of the line, followed by a muffled voice as he asked the same question of his bandmates.

When he came back on the line he said, "I don't, but Jax has a cousin who works there."

She heard Jax yell out, "Cal."

Trent asked, "Why?"

"There's some crap going down here that I can't really talk about. I would, but... I don't want to put you in the middle of it. We need an in over at Riverwoods so we can try to work this out before it turns into a major nightmare." Although, from where Evie sat, it already was.

Silence again.

"Please don't worry about me, Trace," Evie said, trying to keep the tremble out of her voice. The truth was, he should be worried. He should be terrified. After what happened at the gator park, she should be curled up in a ball, falling completely apart. But she wouldn't. She *couldn't* because Dora needed her.

"It's not easy to not worry, Evie," he said gently. "You sound... different. Do you need me there?"

Evie remembered something that made her regret the weak moment when she decided to call him, and she knew she had to do something to prove to Trace she was fine. She found a way to sound confident when she said, "I appreciate that. I really do. But you can't. You have a record label coming to check you guys out tomorrow." She might have wanted Trace by her side, but she loved him too much to ruin his big break, and she added, "Besides, seriously, we've got this handled. It'll probably all be over by the time you could get here anyway."

Trace blew out a breath. "Yeah. We do. I'm nervous, Evie."

She let out a silent sigh, relieved she'd managed to convince Trace she was fine. "Nervous is good, baby. This is a big deal, but you know how those nerves disappear the moment the spotlight hits you? You get that cocky grin and start to strut and—" She let out a small growl of desire.

Trace laughed softly. "Damn it, woman, you make me want to come there to help you out—of your clothes."

Evie laughed. "You're going to be great. I'm sure of it."

"Thanks. I'll call as soon as we know anything."

"I'd love that. Any time of night. I won't care."

"If you're lucky, it'll be a booty call."

She chuckled but her mood sobered, because flirting with Trace was good for her heart but not so good for getting out of trouble. "Can I get Cal's phone number? We need some information to make sure our plan is solid. That would be a tremendous help." She wasn't sure if they'd call him, but she thought it would be good to have the option.

"Sure, babe. I'll get Jax to text it to you."

"You're the best. Good luck tomorrow night!"

After Evie ended the call, her heart felt lighter, and the wave of doom that had settled over her chest had eased. It wasn't a lot, but with a Riverwoods employee's number, at least they had a place to start.

Evie rose from the bed and bounded down the stairs, anxious to give Dora the news.

When Dora saw Evie, she said, "You've got to hear this. Billy was just telling us what he overheard Brian and Jock talking about."

Sunshine jumped into Evie's lap once she sat to listen, and a plate of food thumped before her as Luke set it in front of her.

Billy said, "I was telling them about the fight Jock and Brian had over donating to an animal rescue place."

"Jock does have a thing for animals," Evie said.

"Big enough he was willing to steal for them." Billy gazed longingly at Evie's plate, and she pushed it over to share with him.

"Thanks. I can't believe I'm still hungry after the feast I

already inhaled earlier," he said as he stabbed a piece of beef with his fork. He chewed a bite, and when he swallowed, he got right back to business. "I'm not quite sure on the details but it sounded to me like the two were fleecing old folks at some home."

"Probably Riverwoods," Dora added.

"Jock said he saw the check Mr. Tuttle had given Brian for the animal rescue and that he didn't think he was getting paid enough considering the amount."

"Hold on," Evie said over a mouthful of food. She swallowed it down and asked, "Brian was getting checks from old people at Riverwoods to go to an animal rescue?" She recalled the conversation they'd overheard at the dry cleaners where he was annoyed that Jock wanted to save Sunshine. And the way Brian acted toward her pup, he was no animal lover.

"That's what it sounded like," Billy said.

Evie said, "Well that stinks more than three-day-old fish. How is this tied in with the Franklins? Why would Brian have cared about the flash drive?"

"I have a theory," Dora said. "Think about why one would launder money. So it can't be traced."

"Like by relatives who aren't getting the inheritance they expected," Luke said.

"Right," Dora continued. "Brian was volunteering at Riverwoods and convincing people to donate to *his* animal rescue. Only the animal rescue part of his business doesn't exist. It's a front for his retirement plan. And he needed to wash the money so that it couldn't be traced back to his shell corporation."

"Oh!" Billy said. "The flash drive they were after has that information."

"I bet it does," Evie said as she and Dora locked gazes.

Having that flash drive would be all they needed to put Brian away. It was also what they needed to clear Dora's name and end this crazy adventure. The only problem was the flash drive was on its way to New Orleans. "But we don't have it."

23

The defeated look on Evie's face made Dora want to hug her best friend. She understood exactly how Evie felt, but this latest development was in her wheelhouse, and she was a little bit excited when she said, "We don't actually need it to implicate Brian. All we need to do is find a relative with power of attorney."

"Someone who has access to their elderly relative's finances." Luke said. "Smart."

"Thanks," Dora said as the familiar feeling of pride for being right filled her, like she'd just gotten the best grade in math class. Again. "Then we can find proof of a check to Brian's fictitious animal rescue." She grinned as an even better idea came to her. "In fact, I bet this charity doesn't even have 501c3 status. I know a nasty IRS accountant who'd be perfect to tip off."

"How do we make it happen?" Luke asked.

"For starters, I need the name of the rescue charity."

"Well," Evie said as a smile Dora recognized turned up her lips. "This sounds like we need to scheme, and I have some ideas."

Dora laughed. It was good to have her friend back doing what she did best. And she never thought she think that, but it turned out Evie's scheming ways were darn handy when one was on the run from the law. "I bet you do. Throw them out there."

"Oh boy, here we go," Luke said.

Billy grinned. "Whatcha got, Evie?"

"Well, we need to get close to the Riverwoods residents. We could try infiltrating the dirty-old men population. I know someone who gives a sexy lap"—Evie stumbled over the last word, catching her impulsive utterance too late—"dance".

Dora's cheeks flushed red, horrified Evie had brought it up, and she thought Sunshine was on her side when the little dog let out a growl. Or maybe the pup was ashamed of Dora, too. She dropped her head to hide her face as she mumbled, "I have no idea who you mean."

"Joke!" Evie said quickly in an attempt to cover up her mistake. She let out a nervous laugh. "As if either of us would do something like that. Jeez."

Dora's face was still heated though, and she knocked her fork onto the floor and bent to retrieve it so that her flush would fade before Luke could see it. But as she squatted down to get it, so did Luke. They bumped heads, and she jerked back as stars flashed before her eyes. "Sorry!"

"No, I'm sorry," Luke said. "I've got a really hard head. Are you okay?"

Her forehead right above her left eye throbbed as Dora touched it gingerly, and to her horror she felt a welt already forming. "Yeah. I'll be fine."

When she put her hand down, Luke frowned. "Oh boy, no you're not. I'll get some ice."

When Dora sat back up in her seat, Billy said, "Wow. That's

some goose egg you got there." He frowned. "And it keeps getting bigger."

"Great." Just what she needed on top of everything else that had happened. A third eye like Cyclops.

Evie had the good sense not to stare too hard. "Ouch, Dor." She mouthed, *Sorry.*

You should be, thought Dora, a little peeved that Evie had almost let the cat out of the bag about one of her more embarrassing moments. But when Luke returned and lifted Dora's face with one hand as he pressed a bag of frozen peas to her forehead, she forgave Evie in an instant. It was nice to see the concern on his face. All for her.

"Thanks," she said as she reached up to hold the peas and gazed into his eyes.

He smiled and stroked her cheek with his finger lightly as he removed his hand. They stared at each other for a moment before Billy said, "Maybe you could do a cooking class. What do you say, Luke?"

Sunshine gazed up at Evie and growled.

"Good idea, but that would take a lot of planning," he said. "And approval from the nurses for all the various diets the residents are on."

"Right," Billy said. "I think they all know how to make mashed potatoes and Jello already."

Sunshine let out a yap and pawed at Evie.

"Okay," Evie said as she pushed her dog off her lap. "I think Sunshine needs to go out."

Sunshine didn't head toward the door, though. She moved to the middle of the floor and danced around in a game of chase the tail.

"What has gotten into you, Sunshine?" Evie asked.

"Oh my god." Dora knew exactly what Sunshine was trying to say. "It's so simple; I can't believe we didn't see it."

Sunshine stopped moving to tilt her head at Dora as if to say *It's about time. Goodness people are stupid.*

"Places like Riverwoods love it when people bring in friendly pets. The residents who don't have their own companions enjoy the chance to play with a dog."

Evie patted her legs. "Sunshine!" And when the little dog jumped into her arms, she nuzzled her. "You genius. That sounds like a solid plan." Evie gave Dora with a mischievous look. "Although, not nearly as scheming as I usually like."

Dora grinned. "I know. We should probably wear sensible shoes."

"I don't know," Evie replied. "The stiletto as a weapon wasn't a bad idea."

Dora knew an olive branch from Evie when she saw it and offered one of her own. "Neither was smizing. But really, Evie. How does one actually *smize*?"

Luke and Billy had confused looks on their faces, and Luke said, "I'd like to know how to smize too."

"Fine. I'll show you," Evie said. "Everyone, smile as if I'm going to take your picture."

Billy, Luke and Dora pasted on camera-ready grins, and Evie said, "Now widen your eyes and think about something that makes you really happy. The point is to make your smile genuine.

Dora thought about how nice it had been to have Luke's help, and she glanced over at him. But when he looked back at her with the goofiest looking grin she'd ever seen, she couldn't help it; she burst into laughter. He did the same, and before she knew it, Billy and Evie had joined in.

And while it was probably a release of the day's wild roller coaster of emotions, the truth was they did have something to smile about. They had a plan to take Brian and Marco Franklin down, and there was something about justice that did Dora's heart good.

24

D ora leaned in close to the bathroom mirror to floss her teeth. Evie had gotten ready for bed first, and while Dora could have done so at the same time, she'd spent quality time snuggling Sunshine. She was still shaken up about the drama of the day and needed time to process it.

It was decided that Billy would stay over until they were sure Brian and the mob weren't in a position to do anything to him. Luke set him up in his office with a blow-up mattress for the night. The women were in Luke's room, and Luke planned to sleep on the couch.

In the morning they were going to call Riverwoods to schedule a dog visit with Sunshine for the residents, immediately, if possible. The hope was that they'd find a dog lover who also happened to donate to animal rescue charities. Maybe even Mr. Tuttle who Billy had mentioned. If they were lucky, they'd not only get the name of Brian's charity for the IRS, but they'd also be able to get the name of a relative with power of attorney in order to facilitate getting their hands on a check written to Brian's fake charity for evidence of the scam, which would lead to the money laundering involving the Franklins.

Toothpaste squirted out of the tube as she put it on her toothbrush. The plan sounded solid to Dora. And like something that wouldn't get any of them into hot water since there would be no breaking and entering, no fake personas, and no visits to a shady business dressed in skimpy clothing. But it didn't seem to settle her nerves much. She looked at her toothbrush and sighed. She needed to talk in order to process her day.

Without brushing her teeth, she walked back into the bedroom to chat with Evie. But when she got there, she heard light snoring from both her friend and Sunshine. Evie had a leg hanging off the bed out from under the covers, for temperature control, Dora knew. And Sunshine was curled up in a tiny ball and snuggled into Evie's side.

Dora smiled. It had been a long day for all of them, and she was glad to see they could sleep. She knew that was probably what she needed too, but it wasn't going to come anytime soon. Too much was racing around in her head. Evie called Dora's jumbled thoughts the voices in her head, but Dora refused to use that term since it made her sound crazy. Perhaps a cup of tea would help her relax. She heard Luke rustling around in the kitchen and figured she could make a quick cup before he finally settled down.

She made her way into the kitchen to find Luke must have had the same idea, because he was dunking a tea steeper in a mug of steaming liquid when she walked in. "Hey, there," he said. He lifted his mug up. "Chamomile. Want some?"

"Yes, please."

Luke handed her his ready drink and grabbed a mug from the cabinet for himself. His fancy cappuccino machine hissed as he poured out boiling water into the cup. "Too wired to sleep?" he asked.

Dora sighed. "I am. Evie, however, is passed out with Sunshine. I'm jealous."

"I'm always amazed at people who can sleep no matter what. Stress really affects my ability to get shut eye."

She wrapped her hands around the warm mug, wishing it could take away the chill of her day. Heck, her week. "Me too."

"Come sit with me on the couch." Luke led them over to the living room, and once they sat, he said, "You've been through a lot, Dora. It's no wonder you can't sleep. Are you okay?"

Dora shook her head as tears burned in her eyes. Ever since she'd discovered Marco's money laundering scheme, she'd been on high alert, and it was taking its toll on more than her sleep. She was physically and mentally exhausted but couldn't seem to turn off the fight-or-flight instinct to get some rest.

"Hey," Luke said softly. He set his drink down on the coffee table and leaned back to put his arm up over the top of the couch. "I've got a big, strong shoulder. Lean on it."

Dora nodded and set her tea down before she snuggled into Luke. He wrapped his arm around her shoulders. "Better?"

It was. His T-shirt was soft on her cheek, and his embrace was warm. She realized that if she needed to ball her eyes out, Luke was the kind of guy who'd hold her until she was done. And strangely that made her tears dry up. As if he was already soothing her frazzled nerves with just his touch. He was good at this. She looked up at him. "You have sisters."

He chuckled. "Two younger ones."

"I knew it. You've been way too accepting of me and this situation for anything else to be true."

"What's that supposed to mean?"

"I'm a mess, Luke. A big, awkward, hot mess on a daily basis. Yet you don't seem fazed."

He frowned and shook his head. "Wow. You clearly have no idea how amazing you actually are. Want to know what I see?"

She nodded, curious but a little afraid of what he really thought.

"I see a woman who managed to save her own life doing something nobody should ever have to do because she had no choice. Then she was smart enough to get the hell out of Dodge before someone else tried to kill her. She then discovered someone she trusted wasn't to be trusted at all. With her back up against a wall, do you know what she did?"

"I got my best friend and myself kidnapped."

"You came up with a plan and did some dangerous things to get yourself out of the horrible situation you were thrown into, Dora. And today, even after you were almost gator food, you still were willing to climb into Cecelia's lair to save Billy. You were courageous in a way that impresses me more than you'll ever understand."

"Courageous?" She frowned. "I wasn—"

Luke put his finger on her lips. "Don't you dare let one self-deprecating comment come out of your mouth. You're too smart for that."

That was where she was going to go. It was a knee-jerk reaction she'd cultivated over the years. But it was time to stop doing that. She couldn't afford the luxury of wallowing and self-pity right now. She needed to be at her best, and that meant believing in herself. Dora thought about what Luke had said, and she smiled. Just a little. She had been courageous. Although it was more likely she'd just been too scared to realize how stupid she was being. But she'd take courageous from Luke. And somehow his praise was working to calm her, and she felt a welcome yawn come.

She leaned forward to take a sip of her tea. "You're pretty amazing yourself, Luke." She squinted at him as she wondered again if he'd had some training for the situations they'd been in. "Not only are you a fantastic chef, but you're also capable at lock picking, making realistic sketches, and you have the ability to hypnotize an alligator and a room full of people. I have a feeling there's more to Luke Landucci than most people know."

He winked at her. "Maybe someday I'll tell you my secrets."

Dora dropped her gaze as her heart skipped a beat, and she took a gulp of her tea.

Luke drank too, and then he asked, "Are you hopeful about tomorrow?"

She suppressed a yawn and nodded. "If we could learn something to get both Brian and Marco into trouble with the law, it would sure make this whole thing a lot less scary."

"And then you wouldn't have to leave." Luke set his empty mug down. "Then maybe we could have that date sooner rather than later."

Oh, how Dora wanted to believe it could be that simple. But she had no doubt Marco Franklin wouldn't go down easy. No. She needed that flash drive. "I wish," she said as she set her cup down with a solid thud. "But I'm afraid I need the evidence on that flash drive, and that means I need to go to New Orleans to get it."

"I'll come with you."

It would be so easy to let him. But if tomorrow went as planned, then New Orleans would be nothing more than some convoluted Evie scheme to get a stranger's package in order to retrieve the flash drive. And if it didn't go their way and Brian or Marco somehow found their way to—

She shook her head. She couldn't involve Luke any further into her troubles. "You shouldn't take off from work for this. It'll be a cake walk. And knowing Evie, she's going to want to experience a little Bourbon Street, beignets, and girl time. After the way she's helped me, she deserves it."

Luke frowned but said, "Okay. I'll let you off the hook this time, but I swear to god, Dora, if you find yourself a hot Cajun and ditch me—"

Dora slapped at his chest as she laughed. "And never find out your secrets? Not a chance." This time when her yawn came there was no hiding it. It made Luke yawn too.

He stood up to take their mugs to the kitchen. "Bedtime. For both of us."

Dora stood up, and when Luke turned to her, she said, "Thank you. This was just what I needed."

He smiled. "Same for me. Sleep well, Dora."

"I will. You too, Luke."

25

E vie slowly inhaled the salty ocean air as she waited for Sunshine to do her business. It was early in the morning, but the heat was already settling in as people jogged and walked by, music in their ears or chatting with a friend. She'd woken up before anyone else, and even though people were her thing, Evie was enjoying the quiet. The past three days had been a whirlwind of activity that exhausted even an extrovert like herself.

She thought about Dora, who was conked out in the bed they'd shared last night. She was glad her friend had finally managed to fall asleep. Dora was an anxious person on a good day, and Evie knew that sometimes her friend's mind raced with so much information it was hard for her to make it all stop.

Sunshine gazed up at Evie and wiggled her little fluffy tail as if she wanted to play. "You know what?" Evie asked the pup. "Let's take a little walk to clear our heads. What do you say?"

Evie was barefoot in a pair of the short-shorts and a tank top like those Billy had mentioned to Brian back at the gator farm, and she glanced down at herself, second guessing the wisdom of her walk in what she was wearing. She shook her head because she was afraid Dora was rubbing off on her. Since when did Evie care about what other people thought of her choices? Besides, it was Florida after all, and the heat made it necessary to wear as little clothing as possible. She didn't feel as if she was any more scandalous than women running in sports bras and jogging shorts.

And it was true that she was hardly making a splash when she noticed the people she passed only smiled in a greeting or, in the case of the runners, gave her a sweaty grimace if they glanced at her at all. In fact, it was a little insulting she hadn't turned any heads.

The concrete sidewalk was smooth under her feet as she walked. She did care what Dora thought of her, however, and she grimaced when she recalled how she'd almost told Luke and Billy about her best friend's lap dance. One that had shocked Evie but pleased her as well when she realized Dora was capable of moving way out of her comfort zone to keep them alive.

In fact, she was proud of Dora and the changes she'd been making. Her friend could have easily fallen apart by now, considering all she'd experienced in the last couple of days, and nobody would blame her one bit. But she hadn't.

And that made Evie think she needed to try a little self-growth herself. Starting with keeping her urge to blurt out her every thought in check. As she and Sunshine turned the last corner of the block, she looked down at her adorable puppy. "Sunshine, today is going to be a good day. Let's go save some lives and put away some bad guys. What do you say?"

"Baby, you can lock me up any time!" said a young man who was jogging by her with a friend and had obviously overheard what Evie had said.

She turned to call back to him, pleased she hadn't lost her sex appeal. "I'll do that and give your momma the key!"

His friend elbowed him. "Burn!"

Evie laughed. The smile was still on her face when she let herself back into Luke's townhouse, but it fell when she noticed all the somber faces of her friends who were sitting at the kitchen table. Sunshine let out a questioning whine, and Evie asked, "What's wrong?"

"It's talent show rehearsal day at Riverwoods," Dora said. "No pets allowed, and they won't be until sometime next week."

"And?" Evie glanced down at Sunshine. "Since when has that stopped us?"

"Oh, no," Dora said. "We all know what happened the last time we smuggled Sunshine into some place." She gave the dog a stern look.

Sunshine whimpered and leaned against Evie's leg.

"Hey," Evie said. "She learned a valuable lesson, and I know she'll be good this time."

Luke raised his eyebrows and wisely got up from the table to find something to do in the kitchen, while Billy's head was on a swivel watching the interaction between the women. He definitely found them entertaining judging by the smile on his face.

"No," Dora said. "We can't take any chances with this because I think we're only going to get one shot. It's not a place we can break into."

Evie opened her mouth to give a snippy comeback, but then she remembered her vow for self-growth and closed her jaw so she could give her next words some thought. Dora was right, they probably did have only one chance, and it wasn't like Sunshine had to go. She'd be fine hanging back at Luke's. "Okay. Fine. We do this without Sunshine."

Sunshine let out a whine that sounded a lot like *What?*

Dora blinked a couple times as if she wasn't sure who had taken over Evie's body, but she recovered quickly and sighed. "I guess we have to decide who we're going to be so we have a reason to be let in to Riverwoods."

Sunshine let out a sigh, and her little bones thudded on the hardwood floor when she laid down, resigned to being left out of the mission.

Billy perked up. "You two can be Mr. Tuttle's relatives, and Luke and I will apply for jobs."

Evie exchanged a surprised glance with Dora because that was actually a good idea. Who knew the mailman had a mind for schemes? Maybe he was just the man to help her get Bert Jolen's junkyard collection off his front yard. That stained toilet of his always reminded her of... But that thought was for another time. She said, "That could work."

Dora nodded. "I'll be Ida, his niece."

"Ida?" Evie chuckled. "You sure? Because you can pick any name you'd like, and you want Ida?"

"Hey, it was my great-grandmother's name."

"And that's exactly who should keep it," Luke said as he returned to the table and handed Evie a latte just the way she liked it. "I say you go with something hotter, like *Jessica*."

"Jessica?" Dora asked. "Like Jessica Tandy? Or Jessica Fletcher?"

"Oh, the detective lady on *Murder She Wrote*!" Billy cried. "That's good."

"No," Luke shook his head. "Like Jessica Biel, or Jessica Alba, or"—he pumped his eyebrows at Dora—"*Jessica Rabbit*."

Evie chuckled at the way Dora flushed because of Luke's flirting. "Definitely Jessica for you, and I'll be..." Evie glanced down at her short-shorts. "Daisy, as in Daisy Duke."

Billy nodded in agreement, while Dora said to Luke, "Let me guess. You're going to be James, as in Bond?"

He gave her a smirk. "James works."

"I'll be Clark, like Clark Kent." Billy puffed up his chest. "A hero in disguise."

Evie tried not to spit out her coffee. But she supposed it was appropriate. Nobody would have expected the stout little mailman to have run fast enough to grab his mailbag to protect the mail. "I like it." Her stomach growled as if things were settled, and she hopped up from the table. "What's for breakfast?"

"I'm on it," Luke said as he stood.

Dora got up too. "No. Evie—I mean, *Daisy*—and I can make breakfast. It's the least we can do considering all you've done for us. How would you like your eggs?"

"Scrambled with a little bit of—" Luke stopped himself and shook his head. "I'll take them any way you make them, *Jessica*."

Dora giggled and nearly tripped over herself as she tried to walk backward and turn around at the same time. Fortunately, Evie was there to grab her shoulders and steady her friend. And she was glad to do it, because no matter who they were pretending to be, Dora and Evie made a great team.

26

I t wouldn't be a scheme with Evie if costumes weren't involved, and Dora should have known throwing on a pair of shorts and a T-shirt wouldn't satisfy her friend.

Nope.

"Ta da!" Luke said as he opened two French doors to a huge walk in closet in one of his neighbor's townhouse. Actually, it was more like a room. Dora gaped in awe at the shelves covered with shoes and handbags. Clothing hung on both sides of the room while dressers were on either side of the door. There was even a small riser with a three-way mirror.

"Who is this Erica?" Dora asked as jealousy burned in her gut. She gazed longingly at a Dolce and Gabbana bag.

"Enrique," Luke said. "And he keeps a variety of sizes for his *friends* he brings to vacation with him."

Evie winked at Dora as the situation became clear. She teased Luke, "Do we want to know how you know about this closet?"

Luke chuckled. "I prefer to keep some of my secrets to myself."

. . .

TWENTY MINUTES LATER, Dora had her hair in a high ponytail and was wearing a body-hugging dress with a push up bra that made her look curvier than usual. She put her hand on her stomach that was back to its usual tautness as she gazed at herself in the mirror. There was no trace of too many crab cakes now. Who needed a diet when you were running from the law, a dirty cop, and a crooked former boss? But she drew the line at the wedge sandals Evie pushed at her. She wanted the ability to run if necessary and was wearing practical flats.

Dora glanced in the mirror at Evie, who was beside her trying to tame her wild curls, and said, "All I need to pull this off is some bubble gum to chew."

"Oh! Good one," Evie said as she twisted to check out her backside. She was wearing super-short denim shorts that would have made Daisy Duke proud, and Evie had actually found cowboy boots that fit her, too. "We can stop and grab gum on the way. Now, practice your lines one more time for me."

Dora rolled her eyes and then raised her voice to sound as ditzy as possible. "Hi. I'm, um—" She let out a little giggle. "I'm supposed to visit my great uncle, but—" She let out a little huff. "This is so crazy, but I forgot his name. He's a Tuttle, though. That I'm sure of. Uncle Turtle—" Dora slapped a hand over her mouth. "Oops, don't tell him I said that." She lowered her voice to a whisper. "It's not a very flattering nickname."

"Oh my god, Dora! That was fantastic." Evie yanked on the top of Dora's dress to reveal more of her pumped-up cleavage. "You've got airhead nailed."

"I ought to," Dora groused as she tugged her neckline back up. "I've watched you put on that act for years. And my boobs will stay in my dress. Got it?"

Evie threw up her hands. "Fine."

Dora sighed. She hadn't meant to snap at Evie, and she said, "Sorry. I'm nervous."

"It's okay. I know. And I can take it. Been doing it for years."

Dora smiled at her. "And I'll let you for many more to come."

Evie chuckled. "C'mon. Let's go see if the guys are ready."

They walked back to Luke's, and when they stepped into his living room, Dora stopped in her tracks as her jaw fell open. Billy was in khaki shorts and a polo shirt, but Luke was the one who'd captured her attention. He was in a suit that was tailored perfectly to emphasize his broad shoulders and trim hips. His brow knit as he looked at her. "Dora? Is something wrong?"

"No. I—" She smiled as she shook her head slowly. She didn't have to hide how she felt considering this man had made his interest in her crystal clear. "Not at all, *James*. You're stunningly handsome. That's all."

He grinned as he took in her appearance. "And you, *Jessica*, are stunning as well."

"So, what do you think?" Billy put a foot out to twist his leg and flex his calf. "Do I have the legs of a gardener or what?"

"You sure do, *Clark*," Evie said with an exaggerated southern accent. "I'd hire you based on those legs for sure."

Billy gave her a dramatic bow. "Thank you, *Daisy*." He held out his arm. "Shall we?"

Luke mirrored Billy's action and held out his arm to Dora. "I think we're ready."

Sunshine let out a whine from her perch on the couch, and Dora glanced back at her. "Sorry, girl. Next time. Okay?"

Sunshine let her tongue loll out in reply, and Dora had a sneaking suspicion it was on purpose.

"Be good and we'll bring you a treat," Evie said before they walked out the door.

Dora shuddered as she wondered what was left of Brian after Cecelia was done with him, but Luke had assured her the men would get out of the gator park alive. Even so, she'd checked the local news earlier in the day to be sure, and she hadn't seen anything about half-eaten trespassers.

"Dora! Come on," Evie cried out impatiently from beside Luke's car as Dora walked across the parking lot.

Dora was lagging behind, because every three steps she took, her dress rode up so high on her thighs that she had to stop to yank it down again. "I'm trying!" She let out a huff of frustration and mumbled, "Stupid dress keeps turning into a shirt."

The car beeped as Luke lifted his key fob to unlock the doors. "You could just let it stay there."

She looked up at his amused grin, and her annoyance faded. Because, god, he was even more handsome in sunlight. The way his hair shone... She was a goner. Dora shook her head. She needed to focus instead of getting drooly over a man in a suit. "Next time, you wear the dress and we'll see how you like it."

Luke laughed softly as they finished the short walk to the car. He held her door open so she could slide into the passenger seat in front. Billy and Evie were already in the back.

As they drove to Riverwoods, Evie leaned forward to say, "Dor, open that glove compartment and check out his emergency supplies. Betcha he's got a charcuterie board in there with a split of champagne or something."

Dora laughed. "I'm not going to snoop."

"What? It's one of the best ways to learn about a man. Besides, it's not snooping if he's right here. Luke, tell Dora she can check out your glove box."

"Go for it," he said. His gaze darted to Dora's, and she could tell by the way his lips were twitching he found the situation amusing.

"Okay." Dora did wonder what she might find out about the man. The glove compartment clicked open when she tugged. It was as neatly organized as she'd suspected, and she listed the contents as she pulled them out. "Manual, first aid kit, toothbrush still in its package along with a toothpaste."

"Ooohh," Evie cooed. "The man likes fresh breath. You share an obsession with Dora. If you've got floss too, Luke, she's going to swoon."

He chuckled. "I sure do. Dental appointment party favor. Dig deeper."

True to his word, Dora did find a small container of floss along with his insurance and registration paperwork. But that was all. "Sorry, Evie. No snacks."

"That's because we haven't gotten to the trunk. Maybe that's where he keeps his gourmet picnic."

Luke laughed. "Sorry to burst your bubble, Evie, but in there you'll find jumper cables, a spare tire, and a tire jack."

"Huh," Evie said. "I don't know how you get through life. No change of clothes, no food. All you've got is clean teeth."

"And yet, I'm still here." He winked at Dora.

"Right?" Dora replied as her cheeks flushed slightly. While this banter was fun, she knew Evie was trying to take everyone's mind off the seriousness of what they were about to do. They had one shot to get the information they needed, and while the four planned to split up into two teams to spread a wider net, it wasn't a sure thing they were going to get what they were after.

When they pulled up near the service entrance, Luke and Billy got out go apply for jobs, and Dora got behind the wheel to drive Luke's car through the general visitor's gate. Even from the outside of the property, it was clear the place was well funded. The gate they pulled up to was wrought iron adorned with pelicans, and the man who was sitting in the gatekeeper's house was wearing a pressed white shirt and black hat.

Dora blew out a long breath to calm her nerves before lowering her window to talk to the man. She recited her rehearsed lines, and sure enough they worked. Dora and Evie were one step closer to finding Mr. Tuttle.

The guard said, "I'll buzz you right in, Jessica. You can park in the visitor's lot on the left, and you'll find the club house on the right, across from parking. Someone there will know how to find your uncle for you."

"Thank you so much," Dora cooed in her high voice. She even emphasized her flighty character when she lowered the back window before finding the right button to raise hers. Although, it wasn't an act. She was so nervous that she'd gotten flustered by the controls.

As she drove slowly to the lot, Evie reached over and touched her arm. "You were brill, Dora. We've got this."

Dora turned into a space and clunked the car into park. "Have we, though? Because so much could go wrong, and not only will I be going to jail, but you—"

"Hush." Evie took Dora's face in her hands and looked intently into her eyes. "You just did your part and got us through the gate. Now you can leave the rest up to me if you want. I can sweet talk the igloo off an Eskimo."

Dora laughed. "I'm not sure that's the saying."

Evie laughed too. "Of course, it isn't."

27

Evie was in her element. There was a reason she was able to land so many different jobs. She had the ability to put on a persona and really sell it. Getting through the doors at Riverwoods would be a cakewalk. Or so she thought.

"Well, hello there, sugar," Evie said to the older woman sitting behind the reception desk. "Isn't this place just adorable? No wonder Uncle Tutu loves it so much."

"Uncle Tutu?" Dora muttered in a voice so low only Evie could hear it.

Evie very gently elbowed Dora's side. Now was not the time.

"Can I help you?" the woman asked, peering down her nose and wrinkling it as if she smelled something foul.

"You sure can," Evie drawled, giving the woman a giant fake smile. "We're here to see my uncle Tuttle. We call him Tutu because of that drag queen talent show he was in years ago." She let out a giggle. "You should've seen the way he shook his tush for the audience."

"Vic Tuttle?" the woman asked incredulously. "You can't be serious."

"Serious as a rattlesnake," Evie said, leaning over the counter. "He was a real hoot back in his younger days. I can't wait to see him and give him a giant hug. It's been way too long."

"What did you say your name is again?" the woman asked, punching a key on her computer screen. The expression on her face was sour and full of suspicion.

Oops, Evie thought. *Danger, Will Robinson.* She'd obviously taken a wrong turn somewhere with her commentary. She chewed on the side of her cheek for a moment before saying, "I didn't. Not yet anyway. I'm Daisy, and this is Jessica." She waved a hand toward Dora. "We're actually Tutu's cousins, twice removed, but everyone just calls him Uncle Tuttle... or Tutu in our case. Southern families, I'm sure you understand. My mama insisted we come see him before we left town, and if we leave here without photo evidence of seeing him, she'll chap our hides."

Evie's manic explanation seemed to soften the woman, and her lips twitched into a knowing smile. "Yeah, I know all about southern families, but I can't let you in without Mr. Tuttle approving you as visitors."

Crap on toast, Evie thought. She'd been afraid of that. No matter. Once this Tuttle guy saw them and Dora's cleavage, she was certain he wasn't going to turn them away. "Well, get the old geezer out here then." Her eyes sparkled with mischief. "I can't wait to see if he recognizes us. Both of us have, uh, grown up a bit since he last saw us. I think we were both still in pigtails."

"That's not how we do things—" the receptionist started.

"Peggy," an older gentleman said, appearing in the office doorway behind her. "Go fetch Vic. If anyone could use a visit, it's him. Ever since Puddles passed, he's been a bit more melancholy than I prefer."

"Right." Peggy sent Evie an irritated glance, but she did as her boss asked and disappeared behind the security door.

"Daisy and Jessica, is it?" the other gentleman asked.

"That's right," Evie said, straightening up and puffing her chest out.

He scanned them both and chuckled. "Your names fit you both."

Of course, they did. Evie had seen to that, hadn't she?

"Vic is one lucky man to get to spend the morning with not one, but two young ladies," he said. "Maybe when you're done, you can visit with the veterans. They are always up for—" His phone started to ring, and the man held up one finger, indicating for them to wait.

"Are you sure this is going to work?" Dora asked Evie.

Evie nodded. "If Nurse Ratchet fails us, the dude in the office will get us in."

Dora moved over to the door, trying to peer down the hallway. "Uh-oh. It doesn't look good. Peggy is scowling."

Evie sucked in a breath, wondering which of her lies had been detected. She pulled out her phone and tapped a quick message before hitting Send. "Okay, plan B. Just go with happens next."

"Don't I always?" Dora asked.

Evie placed a hand on her arm. "Yep. It's why I love you so much."

The door flew open, and Peggy strode through, glaring at Evie. "Who are you, really?"

"What?" Evie asked, pretending to be taken aback by the woman's abruptness.

"Mr. Tuttle says he only has a granddaughter and no other relatives. And he's certainly never been called Uncle Tutu," she barked.

Evie continued to act confused, questioning what Peggy had told him and reiterating the family history.

"You're going to have to leave now," Peggy demanded, pointing to the door. "Or I'll have to call security."

"Daisy," Dora started.

"She can't just throw us out!" Evie said hotly. "Mama is going to be really upset if we don't see Tutu. And with her heart..." Evie placed a hand on her chest and sucked in a dramatic breath. "If she thinks Tutu has disowned her then—"

The security door swung open again, and a tall, thin man with spikey blond hair entered the reception area. He had a piercing through his nose and one through his left eyebrow. After casting Evie and Dora approving glances, he turned to Peggy. "Excuse me."

"Cal? What's wrong?" Peggy asked, turning abruptly to the man.

"Nothing's wrong, per se, but Mr. Tuttle is now demanding to see his cousins. Says he can't believe he forgot about his cousin Petunia on his mother's side and that they must be related to her."

"They were close as children," Evie supplied and started to dig around in her purse. "I have a picture right here." She pulled out a faded color portrait of a young boy and even younger girl. They were sticking their tongues out at each other and had mud smeared all over them.

Peggy glanced between Evie and Cal, clearly trying to weigh the situation.

"Just let the ladies in to see Tuttle," the older man barked from his office, sounding exasperated with his receptionist. "What harm could they cause? His biggest danger is having to deal with a woody, and I bet he hasn't had one of those since nineteen eighty-five."

"Mr. Fischer!" Peggy cried, her eyes wide with shock at his outburst.

The older man reappeared again. "Cal, take them on back."

"Yes, sir," the man said. He used his badge to disarm the door and pulled it open. He waved to Evie and Dora. "After you."

The other man turned to Peggy. "I appreciate your dedication to following the rules, but we both know Tuttle is suffering early stages of dementia. If they want to—"

The door slammed shut, cutting off their conversation.

Dora let out a groan. "Dementia?"

Evie joined her friend in her frustration. "That's definitely not going to help us get any information out of Uncle Tutu." She placed a hand on Cal's arm. "Thanks for coming to our rescue. I'm sorry I had to involve you."

"It's no problem. Anything for a friend of Jax's," he said.

"What's going on?" Dora asked.

"Cal is Jax's cousin. You know, from Trace's band? Jax sent me his number, and I gave him a heads-up we might need backup." Evie grinned. "It pays to be prepared."

Dora's eyebrows rose. "I guess so." She turned to Cal. "Is Mr. Tuttle even up for talking to us? If he has dementia symptoms, then I don't think it's wise to agitate him."

Cal shrugged. "It depends on the day. What do you need to talk to him about?"

Evie and Dora shared a look. "Um," Evie said. "It's better if we don't say. It's kinda personal."

He nodded. "I see. Well, you better hurry, because his granddaughter will be here in about a half hour, and if she finds you here and turns you in, the shizzle is gonna hit the fan."

Perfect, Evie thought. That was exactly who they wanted to talk to. "Thanks. We appreciate the warning."

"Sure thing. Mr. Tuttle is at the end of the hall on the right. Stay out of trouble." He winked and disappeared down another hallway.

"We need to tread carefully," Dora said to Evie. "I don't want to upset an older man who isn't totally lucid."

"I know," Evie said. "Let's just find out if he knows anything about a charity first. Then we'll take it from there."

"All right. But no shenanigans," Dora insisted. "If it's true that he's been ripped off, he's been through enough."

"Yes, Mom," Evie said with a roll of her eyes. "I'm not planning on messing with the guy's head."

"I know, but—"

"Lily?" A small woman wrapped her cold hands around Dora's arm. "Oh my goodness. Lily!" Her clear blue eyes lit up with joy and then filled with tears. "You're here. I can't believe it."

Dora cast Evie a panicked glance. Evie started to move forward to help her friend extract herself from the woman's clutches, but before she could even get a word out, a much younger woman with bright red hair and worried green eyes burst from a nearby room, clearly panicked as she scanned the corridor.

"Oh, thank god," the woman said, breathing a sigh of relief. "There you are, Mom. I thought I'd lost you again." She moved over to Dora. "Thank you for keeping her from wandering off."

"She thinks I'm someone named Lily," Dora whispered to her.

"That's her older sister," the woman whispered back. "She passed young, when she was in her thirties." The woman squinted at Dora. "You do kind of look like her." She bit down on her bottom lip. "Would you mind sitting with her for a while? Just let her talk? It calms her to talk to Lily."

"Um..." Dora glanced at Evie.

Go, Evie mouthed. *I've got this.* Evie could tell that wasn't the answer Dora wanted, but the little old woman was clutching Dora's arm so hard and smiling up at her with such joy, it just seemed like the right thing to do. Evie tilted her head toward the redhead. "Ask her if she knows anything about the charity while I go see Tuttle."

"What charity?" the redhead asked.

"Let's talk in your mom's room," Dora said, already letting the older woman lead her through the open door. She glanced back at Evie. "Stay out of trouble."

"Who me?" Evie said, fluttering her eyes in mock innocence. "I'm just a sweet little southern girl. What kind of trouble could I get into?"

Dora snorted and followed the woman and her mother into the room.

28

"I'm sorry, what was your name?" the younger redhead asked Dora. "I don't think I caught it."

"Jessica. And you are?" Dora held out her hand for the woman.

"Darcy. And my mother's name is Augusta, but everyone calls her Aggie."

"It's nice to meet you both," Dora said, perching on a hard plastic chair across from the plain brown couch where Darcy sat with her mother.

"Lily," Aggie sang. "You look so good. You must be using that new-fangled face cream. I swear you just keep getting younger and younger all the time."

"Thank you, Aggie," Dora said kindly to the woman. "That Sephora anti-aging cream is really doing its job."

"I should say so."

She winked at the sweet older lady and said a silent prayer that if she was ever in the same position that someone would indulge her if it meant a visit with a loved one.

Aggie spent the next ten minutes babbling about old stories of her and Lily, trips they'd gone on, old friends they hadn't seen in years, and even touched on old loves that got away. But soon enough the older woman fell silent and started to stare over Dora's shoulder.

Darcy studied her mother and sighed. "I think that's about as much as we're going to get today. She gets tired easily."

"Right." Dora bit back a grimace. She couldn't leave until she asked about Brian and the charity, but even that felt like taking advantage of the older woman. She was in no position to answer any questions, let alone anything about a possible scam. But she could ask the woman's daughter about it. "Hey, Darcy, my friend and I were told there is a man who volunteers here who collects money for an animal charity. Do you know anything about that?"

Darcy's brow furrowed in concentration. "I don't know. Mom did say something about donating to a nonprofit, but I don't remember which one—hold on. Let me take a look at her bank account. I'm sure she wrote a check. She's still old school."

Dora sat back in the chair. "Thanks. I appreciate that. I'm a huge animal lover, and I'm always looking for ways—"

"What in the ever-loving hell?" Darcy shrieked as she jumped to her feet. "Mom, you gave some charity five thousand dollars? We don't have that kind of money. How are going to pay next month's bill for this place?"

Her mother just blinked up at her. "Relax, Mindy. It's only money. Think of the little puppies."

"I'm Darcy, remember?"

"Right, dear," her mother said absently.

Darcy let out a frustrated sigh as a pained look flashed over her face. "Mom, we have to do a stop payment on this check. You can't afford this."

"But Lenny will be so disappointed." She pouted.

"Who's Lenny?" Darcy asked her.

"The one who collected the money," Aggie said.

Dora's heart sank. Lenny wasn't Brian. Was it possible he used a different name when he was working the home? Or did he have a partner in crime?

"Lenny runs the Little Barkers Rehoming charity?" Darcy asked.

"Yes! I always knew he'd grow up to do great things. When we were kids, he was always the one collecting the neighborhood strays." Aggie gave them a bright smile. "Now he can afford to feed them."

Darcy sank back down into the couch. "Oh no." She closed her eyes and pressed a hand to her temple. "She's talking about her younger brother Glen. He passed over forty years ago. That isn't who she gave this money to." Darcy turned to Dora with pleading eyes. "Do you have any idea who took this money? We have to get it back and stop him from doing this again."

"We could look it up online," Dora said, already pulling out her phone. "See who the contact is."

"Of course," Darcy said, breathing a little easier.

Dora found the website easily enough, but as she clicked through the pages, her frown deepened. "There isn't any identifying information or background on here. No phone number or address. Just an email."

"Oh, no." Darcy started to wring her hands together. "That doesn't sound good."

"No, it doesn't. Hold on. Let me try one more thing." Dora quickly pulled up the DNS record. What she found made her eyes bug out. "Surely he can't be this stupid."

"Who?" Darcy jumped up off the couch and ran to Dora's side, squinting at the screen. "Who's Brian?"

"My neighbor," Dora spat out as her fingers flew over the touch screen. She pulled up the Florida government website, searching for the charity registration. There wasn't one. They'd caught him. Mentally, she threw a triumphant fist in the air, but she kept her expression concerned for the sake of Darcy. Brian had five thousand dollars of her mother's money, and unless Brian had the money stashed in his house, she wasn't likely to get it back. "There's no record of this charity being filed with the state."

"And that makes it illegal, right?" Darcy filled in, her expression becoming fierce.

"I should think so."

"Good." She grabbed her own phone and started tapping in numbers. After a moment, she said, "Janelle, we've got a problem. A big one. Mama's been scammed out of some money, and we need to take a jackass down."

Exactly seven minutes later, a tall woman with dark black hair and brilliant blue eyes walked in wearing a sundress. She had a pad of paper in her hand and a scowl on her face. "Tell me everything."

"Jessica, this is my sister Janelle. Janelle, this is Jessica. She helped me figure out this is all a scam," Darcy said.

"I did not get scammed," Aggie insisted from her bed near the wall.

Darcy's nostrils flared as she clearly did everything in her power to hold onto her temper. "Either way, Mama, we can't afford that donation. Janelle is going to deal with it."

"Tell me everything," Janelle said.

Darcy and Dora took turns relaying what they found out, and when they were done, Janelle scowled. "I knew he was dirty!"

"You know that Brian guy?" Darcy asked with a gasp.

"Yeah, he works at the station. I'm going to gather everything I need and then bring his ass down." Janelle glanced at Dora. "You can keep this to yourself for a while, right?"

Alarm bells were going off in Dora's head. Janelle worked at the station? Was she corrupt, too, or could Dora trust her? "I'm not comfortable lying about—"

"I didn't mean to imply you should lie about anything," Janelle said. "I'd never do that. I meant just don't spill that we're onto him so that I have a day or so to make sure I have the evidence I need before I turn his money-grubbing butt in." She glanced down at her notes and chewed on the inside of her cheek, clearly thinking something through. "I knew he was up to something; I just didn't know what."

"Um, sure." What else could Dora say? Nothing. Not until she had that flash drive in her hands. The proof that would keep her out of jail. "Don't worry about me. I don't know—"

"Where is she?" a loud man barked, his footsteps so loud on the tile floors that they seemed to echo through the slightly open door.

"Back here," another man growled. "The little harlot tried charming me right out of my pants."

Dora moved to the door and peeked out. Her heart stopped, and her breath got caught in her throat. It was Brian. His dark eyes were wild and his face beet red as he stomped toward a short, pudgy old man with a bald head.

"No, I did not!" Evie cried. "As if!"

Dora groaned and whispered, "Oh no. Daisy, what are you doing?"

"That limp wanker," Janelle said from behind Dora. "I'm going to enjoy throwing his no-stamina butt in jail."

Again, Dora mentally cheered. She'd like nothing better than to see him rotting in jail. The rat. But she needed to find a way to get Evie out of there. Brian had obviously already spotted her.

Janelle strode out of the door and promptly ran right into Evie. The two bounded off each other, but Janelle maintained her balance while Evie flew backward and landed on her butt with a loud "Oomph!"

"Sorry," Janelle said, barely glancing at her. She moved straight for Brian, a stern look on her face. "Why are you bothering people in an assisted living home?" she demanded.

Brian came to an abrupt stop and glanced around nervously. "I—uh, I volunteer here."

"Right. And I wax every two days." She started to move toward him, but Brian bolted, aiming for the front door.

An older man who'd been on a ladder changing a light bulb chose that exact moment to climb down. He slipped on the last wrung, flung his arm out, and knocked Brian over. He went down in a heap, his head smacking the tile with a loud thunk.

The older man rolled and started to moan as he clutched his arm.

Brian didn't move.

Janelle ran over to Brian and started checking his vitals. Tsking to herself, she pulled out her phone and called for backup and an ambulance. "I've got a runner here. Gonna have to cuff him," she said into the phone. "And chief? He's one of ours. Internal Affairs is gonna need to be let in on this."

Dora stepped out of Aggie's room and grabbed Evie by the arm. "Let's go."

Evie let out a sigh of relief just as the old, pudgy man at the far end of the hallway called, "Hey, Daisy. Don't forget you offered me a hand job. I'll be waiting."

Evie turned around and glared at the dirty old man. "I did nothing of the sort. And if you say anything like that again, I'll tell old Miss Peaches that you have HPV." She stuck her tongue out at him, spun back around and stalked to toward the exit.

"Ha! She's the one who gave it to me," he called back.

Dora shuddered and tried to block out the exchange. All she

wanted to do was get out of there before Janelle figured out she was involved in Steve Franklin's death.

As she passed the handyman, he sat up and winked at her. Dora did a double take when she realized it was Billy. He was wearing a white wig, and she wondered where that had come from. Likely Enrique's closet.

Get out of here, Billy mouthed. *I've got this.*

Of course, he did. The man survived delivering mail in the brutal Florida heat. He could do anything. She gave him a grateful smile and rushed after Evie.

As soon as they were outside, they met Luke at the car and Dora handed him the keys as he said, "Let's go!"

29

"Where are we headed?" Dora asked, squirming in the front passenger seat of Luke's car and tugging at her too short dress again. Evie and Dora had just filled him in on what they'd found out about Brian and that Janelle was arresting him.

"Home. Then you two are getting on the road," Luke said. Evie, while she'd been trying to flirt information out of Tuttle, found out that Brian had gotten money from him, and when Evie tried to point out that it was likely a scam, the old man had gotten belligerent and turned on her. If he came to his senses, that would be two victims that they knew Brian had stolen from.

Dora glanced over at Luke, wondering what he'd been up to while they were getting the dirt. He was wearing blue overalls and dark sunglasses. "Nice disguise."

He chuckled. "Billy and I got the maintenance jobs. Or at least we got a tryout. I think both of us failed. I'm supposed to be dealing with some plumbing right now, and Billy was supposed to be mopping floors, but he got sidetracked by the bad lighting."

Evie snorted. "Can't take direction huh? Hopefully you're better at that in the sack."

"Evie!" Dora shot back. "That's—"

"Funny?" she supplied with a wink.

Dora rolled her eyes and turned to Luke. "How did you know we needed to get out of there?"

"I saw Brian go in. I figured you'd be making a quick escape," he said. A horn blared as they weaved in and out of traffic.

"And Billy?" she asked. "We can't just leave him there."

"Don't worry about him. I'll go back for him." Luke turned a corner, and as Dora braced herself, she was surprised to find they were almost to his house. A few moments later, he opened flipped his visor down and pushed a remote that opened one of many garage doors in a long building Dora had assumed was storage space for the townhome complex residents. When the door was up it revealed a purple convertible.

"Sweet!" Evie said, jumping out of the black sedan and running over to the sporty car. "When did you get this?"

"A few years ago," Luke said. "It belonged to my mother. She gave it to me before she moved up north. Convertibles and snow don't mix."

Dora barely spared a glance at the car, although she did store the information for later. Instead, she hurried inside and straight to the bedroom where she promptly changed into a comfortable pair of shorts and a T-shirt. She'd had just about enough of the short, clingy, wrap dress. When she came out, Luke was waiting for her with a key ring.

Her took her hand in his and gazed down at her with a serious expression. Dora's mind raced with all the things she wanted to say. She wanted to tell him she didn't want to go. Or take him up on the offer to join them. But then she thought about how much danger she'd brought to too many people as it was.

"Here," he said. "You guys take the convertible. You can't be seen in Evie's car. Marco and his gang know what that looks like. And they'd recognize your Toyota, too."

"We can't do that!" Dora insisted.

"The hell we can't," Evie said from behind Luke. She reached over and snatched the keys. "You can take VW that's sitting at the dildo shop and have it as collateral. It will be fine."

Dora sighed. "Evie..."

"We're kind of in a predicament here, Dor. Let Luke do this nice thing." She shoved the key into the pocket of her Daisy Dukes. "I'm gonna go get our stuff while you two say your goodbyes. Be ready to fly in ten."

Dora watched her friend move toward the bedroom, and when she turned back to Luke, she didn't think too hard about what she did next. She threw her arms around him. "Thank you," she whispered in his ear. "I don't know what would've happened to us without you."

"There's no need to thank me, Dora," he said, his voice hoarse. "I don't know what I would've done if something had happened to you."

She let out a small sigh and hugged him tighter.

"I have something else for you." He pulled back and pressed an envelope into her hand.

When she glanced inside, she saw a stack of green bills. "Oh, no. Absolutely not." She shoved it back at him. "This is way too much."

He wrapped his fingers around hers, closing her hand around the envelope. "Don't be stubborn, Dora. Neither of you have jobs, and you can't use your credit cards unless you want to be tracked. Just take it. You can pay me back when you return."

"If we return," she muttered, feeling a little sorry for herself.

"Hey," he said softly, lifting her chin up with one finger.

"You'll be back. All you need is that evidence, and then everything will be fine. Right?"

"Right," she said bravely, forcing herself to smile.

"Good. Now take the cash. You'll need gas and a hotel room. Not to mention road trip food." He winked at her.

Dora resigned herself to the fact that as much as she hated taking his money, she didn't think they had a choice. He was right. They needed cash. She shoved the envelope in her pocket and kissed him on the cheek. "Thank you for everything. I don't think I deserve this but thank you anyway."

"Dora—" he started.

She pressed her fingers to his lips. "Don't say it."

"Can I at least kiss you?" he asked.

She didn't hesitate. Nodding, she stepped a tiny bit closer. Luke tilted his head down and brushed his lips over hers, sending a shiver all the way to her toes despite the summer heat.

"When you get back, I'm taking you out on that date you owe me."

"I can hardly wait."

30

"Whoohoo! New Orleans or bust!" Evie cried into the wind. Not only was she driving the purple convertible with Dora and Sunshine sitting in the passenger seat, but they'd managed to take down Brian and get out of town safely. Luke texted Dora that he'd retrieved Billy without incident, although the man had insisted he had to return at some point to install LED lightbulbs to help the place go green.

While they still had Marco, Fred from the dry cleaners, Jock, and the rest of the money laundering ring to worry about, Evie believed Dora felt as though she could breathe again.

"Hand me those Cheetos," Evie said to Dora. They were about an hour into the trip and had just stopped for gas and junk food.

"You know it's only a three-and-a-half-hour drive, right?" Dora said as she handed over Evie's hard-won treat. Dora had wanted to save their money for nutritious food that would fuel their bodies. Evie had to threaten shoplifting them to get her way. She wouldn't have, of course. But considering the things they'd done the past few days, Dora had her doubts.

"It's still a road trip. Don't harsh my joy." Evie slipped her sunglasses on and sped across the Mississippi State line. "Besides, we'll be home before we know it. That package we sent may have already gotten to Gertie's house."

"I hope so," Dora said. She was quiet for a long moment before she asked, "Does Trace know you've left?"

"Of course not," Evie said, giving her friend a strange look. "Why would I do that? We'll be back tomorrow or the next day at the latest. I don't think Trace will be back before then." It was a lie. Trace would likely be home in a few hours and would come looking for her. A pang of regret filled her. She missed him and hated that she was leaving him in the dark, but she didn't want to pull him into this mess.

"Liar," Dora said softly. "You should call him later and make sure he knows you're thinking about him."

Evie waved a hand and made a *pfft* sound.

"You can't fool me. I know you love him, even if you can't seem to make a commitment," Dora said as she patted Sunshine's head.

"It's just not the right time to commit," Evie said, sounding annoyed. "We're off to New Orleans, he's performing, and... I just don't think I'd do well with a ring on it, if you know what I mean. I'm too much of a free spirit."

"That might be true," Dora said with a nod. "But I still think you two are perfect for each other."

"Just like you and Luke," Evie said with a knowing smile. "You two are gonna make gorgeous babies someday."

Dora turned away, but not before Evie saw her cheeks flush pink.

"It was hard to leave him, Evie," Dora said. "I've never had a man be so sweet to me before."

Evie's heart swelled as she glanced at her friend, happy that she'd finally found someone who made her feel so special. But in true Evie fashion, she gave her friend a giant smile and said, "I know, sweetie. But don't worry, you still have me! And New Orleans is gonna be lit! You'll see."

Dora glanced at her friend, chuckled, and then threw her head back and called, "New Orleans, here we come!"

The sun was setting low in the sky when Evie pulled the car into the parking lot on North Peter's street. The French Quarter was alive with street performers and tourists while off-key music blared from the calliope on the nearby steamboat. Energy filled the air, and once they were out of the car, Evie stretched her arms out wide, happily twirling around. "I love it here!"

Dora wasn't quite so giddy. She glanced at her phone, frowning. "Let's just find Gertie."

"Relax," Evie coaxed, clipping the leash onto Sunshine's collar. "Her apartment is just around the corner. We'll stop there first, then head to Bourbon Street. By tomorrow night you'll be back in Luke's arms."

Dora rolled her eyes at her friend. "I'm not worried about Luke. I'm worried about evidence."

"And that's why you're so uptight." Evie slipped her arm through Dora's and started to tug her down the uneven sidewalks. "Do you smell that?"

"What? The stench of rotten oranges?" Dora asked.

"No, party pooper. Beignets! As soon as we meet Miss Gertie, we're heading to Café du Monde, and then we'll do Bourbon Street and get a couple of hurricanes. We'll find somewhere fabulous for dinner and—"

Dora stopped them short. "Please tell me I'm not seeing what I think I'm seeing," she said with a gasp.

Evie's heart skipped a beat. "You don't see two ambulances and four police cars," she said with the hope it could make it true. The building directly in front of them was where they were headed. "Or that stretcher being rolled out of the building."

"No. This isn't happening. Oh god, what if ..." Dora said, pressing her hand to her stomach.

"There's only one way to find out." Evie tugged Dora up to the small group of bystanders who were talking in hushed voices. "Excuse me."

A little old woman with short, brassy blond hair turned to look at them. "Yes, dear?"

"Can you tell us what happened here? We're supposed to meet our Great Aunt Gertie and—"

The woman let out a small sob, clasped her hand to her mouth, and shook her head as tears sprang to her eyes. "You poor dears."

"That wasn't..." Dora gulped.

"It's Gertie," The woman cried. "My sweet Gertie. She was fine this morning. And now she's dead."

Evie and Dora gazed at each other in shock. It was one thing to sweet talk an old woman into opening a Buddha-shaped piggy bank so they could get a flash drive. But one who was dead?

A tear rolled down Dora's face, and, to be honest, Evie wanted to cry too. She didn't, though. She grabbed Dora's hands and looked her hard in the eye. "We've got this, Dor. You'll see."

The End

WHY DO Dora and Evie want beignets, étouffée and a Budda bank? Follow them to New Orleans to find out in *Mischief in New Orleans.*

ABOUT THE AUTHOR

Lucy Quinn is the brainchild of New York Times bestselling author Deanna Chase and USA Today bestselling author Violet Vaughn. Having met over a decade ago in a lampwork bead forum, the pair were first what they like to call "show wives" as they traveled the country together, selling their handmade glass beads. So when they both started writing fiction, it seemed only natural for the two friends to pair up with their hilarious, laugh-out-loud, cozy mysteries. At least they think so. Now they travel the country, meeting up in various cities to plan each new Lucy Quinn book while giggling madly at themselves and the ridiculous situations they force on their characters. They very much hope you enjoy them as much as they do.

Deanna Chase, is a native Californian, transplanted to the slower paced lifestyle of southeastern Louisiana. When she isn't writing, she is often goofing off with her husband in New Orleans or playing with her two shih tzu dogs.

Violet Vaughn lives on a small island off the coast of Maine where she spends most mornings walking along the water with her Portuguese water dogs.

www.lucyquinnauthor.comlucy@lucyquinnauthor.com

ALSO BY LUCY QUINN

Secret Seal Isle Mysteries

New Corpse in Town

Life in the Dead Lane

A Walk on the Dead Side

Any Way You Bury It

Death is in the Air

Signed, Sealed, Fatal I'm Yours

Sweet Corpse of Mine

Knocking on Death's Door

Highway to Homicide

Accidentally Undercover

Peril in Pensacola

Mischief in New Orleans

more to come...

Made in the USA
San Bernardino, CA
05 August 2019